THE COPPER-DUN STUD

Ray Hogan

GUNSMOKE

This hardback edition 2005
by BBC Audiobooks Ltd
by arrangement with
Golden West Literary Agency

ISBN 1 4056 8054 7

British Library Cataloguing in Publication Data available.

Printed and bound in Great Britain by
Antony Rowe Ltd., Chippenham, Wiltshire

THE COPPER-DUN STUD

When a pair of dangerous outlaws shot Amos Cord and stole his prize horse, they didn't reckon on coming up against Tom Medley. But Tom found the old man just in time and lit out on the trail of the no-good varmints.

Yet soon the horse thieves were the last thing on Tom's mind when he found himself caught between a desperate woman, Lucilla Kinkaid, and the three vicious gunmen pursuing her. As he and Lucilla rode into a bullet-blazing ambush, Tom realized helping her might cost him far more than the chance of getting Amos's copper-dun stud back—it might just cost him his life!

Ray Hogan is an author who has inspired a loyal following over the years since he published his first Western novel *Ex-marshal* in 1956. Hogan was born in Willow Springs, Missouri, where his father was town marshal. At five the Hogan family moved to Albuquerque where Ray Hogan still lives in the foothills of the Sandia and Manzano mountains. His father was on the Albuquerque police force and, in later years, owned the Overland Hotel. It was while listening to his father and other old-timers tell tales from the past that Ray was inspired to recast these tales in fiction. From the beginning he did exhaustive research into the history and the people of the Old West and the walls of his study are lined with various firearms, spurs, pictures, books, and memorabilia, about all of which he can talk in dramatic detail. Among his most popular works are the series of books about Shawn Starbuck, a searcher in a quest for a lost brother, who has a clear sense of right and wrong and who is willing to stand up and be counted when it is a question of fairness or justice. His other major series is about lawman John Rye whose reputation has earned him the sobriquet The Doomsday Marshal. 'I've attempted to capture the courage and bravery of those men and women that lived out West and the dangers and problems they had to overcome,' Hogan once remarked. If his lawmen protagonists seem sometimes larger than life, it is because they are men of integrity, heroes who through grit of character and common sense are able to overcome the obstacles they encounter despite often overwhelming odds. This same grit of character can also be found in Hogan's heroines and, in *The Vengeance of Fortuna West*, Hogan wrote a gripping and totally believable account of a woman who takes up the badge and tracks the men who killed her lawman husband by ambush. No less intriguing in her way is Nellie Dupray, convicted of rustling in *The Glory Trail*. Above all, what is most impressive about Hogan's Western novels is the consistent quality with which each is crafted, the compelling depth of his characters, and his ability to juxtapose the complexities of human conflict into narratives always as intensely interesting as they are emotionally involving. His latest novel is *Soldier in Buckskin*.

1

Tom Medley drew the bay horse he was riding to a halt at the edge of Amos Cord's yard. Something was wrong. A heavy silence hung over the place, one broken only by crows cawing in the distance. Ordinarily Amos would be seen out by one of the many corrals that made up the horse ranch, but there was no sign of him. Nor was there any indication of Ike Trigg or Rufe Donner, the old man's two hired hands.

True, the area was not deserted; Tom could see several mares in the holding corral, and on beyond the small scatter of outbuildings, in the fenced yard reserved for such, were a number of mustangs that still needed work and training before they could be sold either to the army, or to one of the livery stables, or to other buyers. He could not see into the barn from where he was, but like as not the animals requiring special care were in their stalls as usual.

It was Tom Medley's habit to stop by his old friend's ranch once or twice a week just to say howdy and to see if Amos—a man now well up in his sixties and suffering patiently all the numerous aches and pains of poorly knitted broken bones and battered muscles that came from a lifetime of dealing in horseflesh—was all right.

Tom's own ranch was on the opposite side of a ridge deep in the heart of the Mogollon Mountains in southwest New Mexico Territory, so it was never any big chore to drop in on Cord when he was out looking after his herd, small in number now—less than a hundred head, in fact—but growing. Given a few more years of good grass and water, and no severe winters, and he'd be on top of the world, Tom figured, thanks to Amos Cord.

Searching the premises visible to him once more with careful eyes, Medley backed the bay gelding a few steps, and cut left. Circling to the south, he came in on the blind side of the small house in which Amos Cord lived alone. Halting in the dense windbreak of oak brush, Medley dismounted quietly and, tying the bay to a stout branch, drew his gun and began to make his way toward the hut.

Tension and apprehension were mounting higher within him. He could still neither hear nor see anyone. The bunkhouse where Trigg and Donner lived, a somewhat newer and better structure than Cord's own quarters, was only a short distance away, across the hardpack. Its door was standing open, and there was no one about.

Somewhere on the other side of the barn one of the numerous horses in a corral began to kick up his heels and race about for some reason. Tom listened for a brief time, waited to see if Trigg or Donner or perhaps Amos Cord would appear to investigate the cause of the disturbance, but there was no reaction from any quarter.

Grim, Medley turned the corner of the hut and moved silently and slowly for the door. He stopped short. The heavy panel was closed. That, too, like the eerie quiet that hung over the ranch, was unusual; at that near noon time of a late-spring day Amos Cord would have had his door open, allowing the warm air to fill the cabin. Continuing, Tom reached the entrance and halted while he waited out a long minute, ears straining for an alien sound. Hearing none, he grasped the handle, pressed the thumb latch, and weapon up and ready, pushed open the thick panel.

The hinges creaked loudly, bringing Tom to an abrupt halt. The squeal of the dry metal would have been heard not only throughout the two-room house, but in the yard as well. It brought no response, however, and taut, Medley stepped into the familiar room.

It was a combination of kitchen, dining room, parlor, and office. Tom had been in it often drinking coffee, or maybe having something a little stronger from the jug Amos kept on the shelf adjacent to the stove, while they talked over ranch problems, the weather, the condition of the grass in the Mogollon country, or maybe just discussing a bit of gossip passed on by someone riding up from the nearby town of Waggomann.

Crossing to the stove, Tom laid a hand on its flat, four-lid surface. It was cold. So was the battered old granite coffeepot that had seen so many years of service. Frowning, Medley drew back into the center of the room.

A man in his late twenties, Tom was a lean, rawboned man with a hard-set mouth overhung by a full mustache. He had dark hair and eyes that seemed perpetually narrowed as if from looking too long into the sun. For most of his life he had been a drifter—coming from everywhere going nowhere, with no aim in life until he encountered Amos Cord, who had changed his outlook and given him something to live for.

Pivoting slowly on a heel, Medley faced the door that opened into Cord's sleeping quarters. If Amos wasn't in there, he thought—and then checked himself at the outrageous idea; the old man wouldn't still be in bed unless, of course, he was sick or had been hurt. But if that was so, why weren't Donner or Trigg around looking after him?

Tom swore angrily. He'd never had much use for Cord's two hired men. They had shown up one day about six months previous flat broke, hungry, and needing a job. Amos, as usual, had taken them in; he was always throwing open his door to someone who was having it rough—a failing or a quality that, Tom had warned the older man on several occasions, he might eventually regret.

"I ain't never been sorry I gave you a helping hand." Amos had grinned.

Tom had wanted to reply that not every man would be as appreciative as he, but he'd kept quiet. Saying it just didn't sound right—and he'd been wrong about Trigg and Rufe Donner, so far at least. The pair had worked out well, especially Rufe, who had proved to be particularly good with livestock.

"There's some fellows that horses take right to," Cord had told Medley one evening when they were riding into Waggomann to see about some feed Amos had ordered. "And there's them that no matter what a horse just won't ever cotton to. Now Rufe's the first kind. He's got the knack or whatever it is that makes them trust him. I've seen him walk right into a corral where there's a stallion just a-honing to kick and bite somebody to death. But not Rufe. The damn stud'll make right up to him and be as gentle as an old maid's buggy mare."

Medley's wide shoulders stirred beneath the heavy linsey-woolsey shirt he was wearing as he brushed the remembrance of Cord's words from his mind. He'd been pleased that Amos had found some good help, but that had nothing to do with the present moment—for there sure as hell was something wrong.

Thumb hooked over the hammer of his forty-five, Tom crossed quietly to the bedroom. Glancing over his shoulder at the sunlight-flooded backyard once more, and seeing no one, he pushed open the door to Cord's sleeping quarters.

An oath ripped from his lips as anger and concern flooded through him. Amos Cord lay face-down on the floor. There was a crusted bloodstain between his shoulders, and more dried blood on the faded, worn carpet near his head.

2

Grim, Tom Medley knelt beside the elderly rancher. Who would want to hurt Amos Cord—a man who constantly went out of his way to show kindness and lend a helping hand to anyone down on his luck?

Grasping Cord by a shoulder, Tom gently turned the older man onto his back. The oldster's eye lids fluttered and opened. Medley heaved a deep sigh of relief. He had been certain Amos was dead. Thankfully he had been wrong, but Cord was in a bad way, there was no doubt of that.

"Tom?" Cord's voice was barely audible despite the hush.

Medley, holstering his weapon, carefully slipped his arms under the rancher's shoulders and legs, lifted him off the floor, and laid him on the bed.

"It's me all right, Amos," he said. "Looks like you've had a mite of trouble."

Cord moved his head slightly. He was almost

11

too weak to speak, Tom realized, and then it occurred to him that his old friend could have been lying there on the floor helpless for several days. Wheeling, Tom returned to the kitchen, quickly built a fire in the range, and removing one of the stove lids, set the half full pot of coffee over the open flames. The brew was old, and heated to a boil again, it would be strong—which was just what Amos Cord needed. Meantime a drink of water and a swallow or two from the jug would help.

Pouring a tin cup half full of the liquor, and taking up a dipper of water from the bucket on the counter beyond the now rumbling stove, Tom returned to the bedroom. Cord's eyes were open, and he stared up at Medley with a half-smile on his colorless lips.

"I-I reckon I ain't in such good shape," he said haltingly as Tom held the dipper to his mouth.

Medley shook his head in agreement. He was noting the dark bruises about Cord's face and neck and the places where the skin had been broken. Not only had the rancher been shot, once in the back, but badly beaten about the head as well. The anger that had dwindled at finding his old friend alive swelled through Tom once more.

"Who the hell did this to you, Amos?" he demanded in a hard voice.

Cord, finished with the water, motioned feebly at the cup of whiskey. Tom raised it to the old man's lips, waited while he swallowed slowly and laboriously. He was wondering if he shouldn't do

something about the wounds Cord had sustained—
clean them and apply whatever medicine he might
find, and bandage them, perhaps. But the bullet
wound and the cuts in his face and neck were no
longer bleeding, and to fool with them could start
them flowing again. Best he leave treatment for
the doctor, he reasoned, since there was no longer
any danger from the loss of blood.

The tin cup drained, Amos pushed it away. He
seemed to settle back, become more relaxed. A
brightness now glowed in his dark, deep-set eyes
and his voice was stronger when he spoke.

"Sure lucky—you took a notion to come by—"

Tom smiled and repeated his earlier question.
"Who jumped you, Amos?"

Cord stirred. "Was Rufe—Ike Trigg."

The two hired hands! Medley swore harshly. He
hadn't liked them from the start, guessed now his
feelings were well-founded.

Amos gave that thought, his usually ruddy but
now ashen features knotting into furrows.

"Yesterday morning—I reckon it was. Or maybe
it was the day before. I just ain't for certain—"

The coffeepot began to rumble and a faint hiss-
ing arose as the liquid inside it started to boil.
Cord paused.

"That coffee I'm smelling?"

Tom nodded. "Sounds like it's ready."

"Could sure use a swallow or two—and a bite of
that roasted venison you'll find in the window
box." Cord hesitated again, took a labored breath.

13

"Some cold biscuits in the oven. Be obliged if you'll fetch me a couple of them, too. I'm a speck hungry," he finished.

Medley felt a measure of relief course through him. It was a good sign; a dying man ordinarily didn't complain of being hungry. Hurrying into the kitchen, Tom sliced off a bit of the venison roast, put it on the plate with several biscuits, and set it on the stove to warm while he obtained another cup to fill with coffee. He was amazed at Amos Cord's condition. The old man had the constitution of a mule—lying wounded and bleeding on the floor for one, possibly two days, and now ready to sit up and take nourishment! By all the usual standards he should be dead.

Filling the cup with the strong, black liquid from the pot, and taking up the plate of meat and biscuits, Medley retraced his steps into the bedroom. There was a straight-back chair against the wall close by, and handing the coffee to Cord, Tom dragged it up beside the bed where it could serve as a table.

"This is mighty powerful coffee," Amos murmured, sipping from the cup. "I've come across sheep-dip that weren't bad as this—"

"You made it," Tom cut in, grinning as he set the plate of food on the chair. "Don't know when. Was already in the pot."

With each passing minute he was feeling better about his old friend. Amos was apparently going to be all right despite having been shot in the

14

back and the beating he'd taken about the head. He'd go for the doctor, anyway, just to be sure. The bullet hole would need attention even if it no longer bled.

"Them damn yahoos," Amos said, chewing on a piece of the meat, "they snuck up behind me, walloped me good on the head. When I made a grab for my scattergun, that's when one of them plugged me. Think it was Ike Trigg but I ain't for sure."

"Why? What'd they want?"

"Money—and that stud of mine, the copper dun—"

Tom stared at the older man. "They took him— that big stallion?"

"Was the main thing they was after," Cord replied. "Money—hell, all I had was maybe fifty dollars. The stud was what they wanted. Heard Donner tell Ike that he knew a rancher in Abilene, Texas way, that'd give a thousand dollars for a horse like him."

Amos' voice had trailed off, and the hand in which he was holding the bit of meat sank to his side as strength abruptly ebbed. He lay motionless for several moments, and then once more began to chew on the venison and munch at a biscuit.

"Reckon I've got to do something I ain't never done before, and sure ain't proud of," Cord said after a time. "I'm calling in that favor you owe me, Tom. Wouldn't do it if I had any other way to turn."

"You know damn well how I feel about that, Amos! All you've got to do is tell me what you want and I'll do it."

"I'm asking you to light out after them two, get the copper dun back. I don't care nothing about the money, but that there stud—well, he's my whole dang life! I ain't got nothing worth a bucket of dust, 'cepting him."

Tom Medley, silent, nodded. He was remembering how Amos scrimped and saved and got by just so as he could purchase the copper dun—some folks termed him a bronze chestnut—while only a colt. The old man's intuition and sound knowledge of horseflesh had said the colt had the makings of a magnificent animal—and he had been dead right. There was no finer-looking or stronger stud in the whole country than the copper dun; Amos had named him appropriately, Copper.

"I know this ain't no time for you to go gallivanting off, leaving your place—what with calves to brand and strays to roundup—and believe me, Tom, I wouldn't if—"

"Forget it," Medley broke in. "I've got Earl Craig's boy helping me out. He won't be able to do all that needs doing, but he can keep an eye on things while I'm gone. Hell, Abilene ain't so far—"

"Right—and I don't figure Ike and Rufe'll be pushing hard. Instead they'll be going careful like with the stud, not wanting to get him skinned up or leaned out any."

16

"Ought to be easy to follow, too. Man don't see a horse like that very often."

Cord managed a nod. "Maybe not even more'n once in a lifetime! Was all set to start breeding him to them chestnut mares I've got penned out back—figuring to come up with some real fine animals that, in a couple of years, could be put together for matched teams. They'd bring a pretty penny, but now I'm wondering if I'd best forget—"

"No need—I'll bring the stud back to you," Tom said. "You want some more meat and biscuits? Coffee?"

"If I've got my druthers, I'll just have another pass at that jug—"

"Sure," Tom said, and getting the liquor, filled the old rancher's cup and set the crockery container on the chair where it would be within reach. "Expect I'd better ride into town, get Doc Masters, then fix to ride out—"

"The doc can wait. Couple hours more ain't going to make no difference one way or other. I'd be mighty obliged if you'll first take a look at the horses. Expect Rufe left them with water and feed, him being that kind, but I'd feel easier if I knew for certain he had. Them chestnut mares in the holding pen—I sure don't want them suffering none. Same goes for them horses in the barn. They'll be foaling in a few days and they ought to be looked in on. You can open the gate of the big corral, turn them broomtails out to pasture. And then—"

Medley waved the older man to silence. "I'll go have a look at them all and do what's needful. You just lay there and take it real easy till I get back."

Cord signified his satisfaction with a faint smile, "Saying again I'm sure glad you come along. Them horses all would've got in a bad way if they'd run out of water and feed."

Medley agreed and, leaving the room, headed out across the hardpack for the collection of corrals and other structures. It was like Amos Cord, in a bad way himself, to worry about his stock.

The mares were restless and trotted nervously back and forth within their enclosure when he approached, but they settled down quickly when Tom filled their water trough and pitched in some fresh hay from a pile conveniently nearby. Their grain boxes, affixed to one side of the corral, were empty also, and after locating the sacks of oats in the barn, Medley replenished the wooden containers as well.

That completed, he saw to the pregnant mares, throwing down fresh timothy from the barn's loft, refilling the mangers in the stalls and the half-barrels of water sitting in the runway. None of the mares appeared or acted ready to foal so he reckoned he need not worry about that.

Moving on to the large, fenced-in yard where a dozen mustangs milled about, he opened the gate and let them race out into the open field, where they immediately began to graze. They would require no further attention as there was plentiful grass on the gently rolling slopes and ample water in the creek that flowed through the pasture.

Returning then to the house, he reported on conditions to Amos Cord, who listened attentively, a smile on his thin lips. When Medley was finished, he nodded.

"Knowed I'd never made no mistake with you, Tom."

"Just don't you ever forget that I'm owing you plenty for what you done for me," Medley said. "Now, expect I'd best be getting on my way. Sooner I start trailing those horse thieves, the better."

"I ain't afeard you won't catch them—and when you do, you know how to handle them. Just be real careful with the stud—"

"Can bank on it. I aim to stop by my place first, get my trail gear, and go on into town, find Doc Masters, and send him out here to fix you up."

"Ain't no big hurry there. Just you leave that jug handy. And maybe a little more of that venison."

Tom obtained the meat and several biscuits and placed them on the chair near the bed—along with the jug of liquor.

"Oughtn't to take me more'n a couple of weeks if I have to follow Trigg and Donner clear to Abilene," he said, taking Cord's hand into his own and giving it a firm squeeze. "Be back sooner if I get lucky."

"Like I was saying, I expect they're taking it slow," Cord reminded Medley. "They won't be in no hurry 'cause they figured I was dead when they rode out. And with money in their pockets they'll be visiting every saloon along the trail . . . One thing, Tom," the rancher added, pausing for a deep breath, "best you watch out for Ike Trigg. Fancies hisself a sort of gunman. Rufe Donner's pretty good with his iron, too."

"I'll take care of them—don't you fret none over that, you just see to getting back on your feet. I'll be coming back with that copper-dun stud of yours along with the hides of both Rufe Donner and Ike Trigg."

Cord grinned. "Hell, don't bother none with them. Can just leave them laying alongside the trail for the buzzards and coyotes to take care of—far as I give a dang. It's the stud that's important to me . . . Good luck."

"Obliged, and good luck to you, Amos," Tom said, and returning to the yard, made his way to where the bay was waiting. Mounting up, he struck out across country for his own ranch.

3

Young Andy Craig was herding a small jag of steers onto new grass when Medley, having avoided the road in the interest of saving time, cut diagonally across his south range and encountered the boy. Signaling to Andy, he drew into the shadow of a tall spruce and waited for him to ride up on the small pinto pony he preferred to use.

"Amos Cord's been hurt, and robbed," Tom said as the Craig boy, the usual smile on his round face, halted before him. "Those two hired hands of his shot him, then rode off with what money he had and that big copper-dun stud he set such store by."

"They stole him—that stud?"

Medley nodded. "I'm going after him—Amos asked me to. Means you'll have to look after things around here for me."

"How long'll you be gone?"

"Two weeks, maybe a bit more—and it could

21

take less all depending on how soon I can catch up with Rufe and Ike."

Andy Craig's smiled widened at the prospect of being in sole charge of Medley's ranch for such a period of time.

"Well, don't you worry none about things here at the T-Bar-M," he said, mentioning Tom's brand. "I'll for sure take care of everything."

"I'll be obliged if you will—and if you need some help, maybe you can get one of your brothers to pitch in, give you a hand. I'm willing to pay the same wages as I'm giving you."

"Sure, maybe, but I ain't exactly certain Pa'll—"

"I'll leave it up to you. One thing, I want you to round up the calves, put them in one of the corrals so they can be ready for branding. Be sure you find them all—likely be a few hiding out in that brush along the creek."

"Seen a couple down there just this morning," Andy volunteered promptly.

"Was aiming to hand-pick twenty-five of the best steers and drive them over to J. P. Willard's for shipping. He was going to include them in his herd, save me making a drive to the railhead."

"You want me to do that?" Andy asked eagerly.

Tom gave it thought. He needed the money the sale of the steers would bring, and since Willard, who ran a large spread some miles to the east of him, planned to get his drive under way that weekend, it would be too late to take advantage of Willard's kind offer when he returned from

Abilene—if he had to go that far. The only logical answer was to let Andy Craig take care of that, too.

"Reckon I'll have to. Cut out twenty-five head and get them over to Willard. He's expecting them. You can tell him why I couldn't bring them myself."

Andy bobbed happily. "Maybe I better rope in my kid brother. He ain't but twelve, but he can ride real good and he'll do what I tell him. Where you headed now?"

"By the house. Got to pick up my blanket roll and trail gear."

"You want me to drop by old ma—Mr. Cord's place and look in on him?"

Medley shook his head. "No need—and I expect you'll find yourself plenty busy here on the ranch. I'll be stopping in town as I ride out. Aim to send Doc Masters to take care of Amos, maybe bring along somebody to stay with him till he gets back on his feet."

The boy whistled softly. "You sure do think a lot of Mr. Cord, Tom—going off and leaving your ranch right now when there's a powerful lot of things that need tending to."

"I owe him," Medley said simply, and turning away, rode on.

Owe Amos Cord more than I'll ever be able to pay, Tom thought as he put the bay into a steady lope. I'd be rotting in the bone yard right now if it wasn't for him.

And it was a debt—not just a favor as Cord had

put it—that always stood foremost in Tom Medley's mind. He'd been on the trail for years knocking about, drifting back and forth from Paso del Norte on the southern border to Montana's Bozeman in the north; he'd had his look at the cattle slaughter capital of the world, Chicago, to the east, and seen the big canyon of Arizona Territory in the west, and never once given a moment's consideration to the future—to settling down.

It was a wasted way of life, Tom knew; even saloon girls on occasion had pointed that out to him. But he'd shrugged it off. What the hell difference did it make how a man spent his days? Nobody ever got out of this life alive anyway.

Then came that night in a Silver City saloon. Well liquored up, he was sitting in on a game of poker with four other men, a whiskey peddler, two miners, and a tinhorn. He'd just come off big winner in a game up in Colorado's border town of Trinidad, and now, with one of the casino's prettiest girls on his knee, he was thoroughly enjoying a run of good cards.

All came to a sudden stop when he saw the gambler palm a card. Tom called up the sharp's hand; there was instant gunplay. Hindered by the need to get the girl on his knee out of the line of fire, he was late drawing his weapon and consequently took two bullets in the chest and one in the shoulder from the tinhorn's belly gun before he could trigger his forty-five. He fired three times: the first shot killed the gambler, the second a man standing beyond, the third bullet buried itself in the ceiling as he himself sank to the floor.

It was the saloon girl who helped him rise, took him to her room, and doctored him as best she could, all the while telling him he must get out of town immediately as the man he had killed accidentally was a member of a large family of hardcase miners and they'd not accept any explanation pertaining to the death of their kin.

Heeding the girl's advice, Medley had ridden out in the dead of night on a trail that led north into the towering Mogollon Mountains, although he was entirely unaware of that fact. He had pressed on for hours half-conscious, again bleeding profusely and all but falling off his horse, which he eventually did.

Tom had regained consciousness on a bed in a small house; an elderly man bending over him had said his name was Amos Cord. His wounds had been cared for once again, and despite a vague sort of perception, he was resting comfortably.

Cord had found him lying on the trail more dead than alive that morning. The rancher had carried him to his shack where he did what he could to save what little life still flowed through Medley's body; later, when three riders came by looking for a man who had killed their brother, Cord had denied seeing anyone and had sent them on their way. Thus Tom Medley felt he owed his life to Amos Cord—not once, but twice.

It hadn't ended with Amos nursing him back to

good health. They'd held long talks about life, and living it the way a man should; they had agreed that each had an obligation to himself to do something for the good of others, even if in a small way—and not be just a void during his allotted time on earth.

Amos had suggested Tom get in the ranching business in one way or another, raising either cattle or horses. Cord said he could understand why mining was out—he himself couldn't live a single hour digging in a dark hole in the ground. Since Tom didn't have the love for horses that Amos had—the love that it took to be a success in raising them—he thought a cattle ranch would be the best bet. There was a small place on the other side of the ridge, he recalled, that could be had for little more than a song.

Tom had followed Amos Cord's advice. He'd bought the ranch from the people who owned it for an even two hundred dollars, which was a fair-enough price, for the place consisted of only a half-section of land, a homesteader's cabin, and a couple of sheds. He'd had little cash left after that but was able, through Cord's connections, to get his hands on a few steers, cows, a couple of bulls, and lay in a stock of grub before he was flat broke.

After that it had been nip and tuck with bankruptcy, but this year things were looking up. Beef prices were good, his calf crop had been better than average, and it appeared that for the first time—after selling off the twenty-five steers—he'd have a little extra money. But he needed to watch matters close, and to do that he must get back to the ranch as soon as possible. He couldn't afford to lose a single head of cattle.

Tom's thoughts along such lines came to a stop as he reached the edge of his yard and turned in. Moving fast, he entered the two-room shack that served as home, grabbed up his saddlebags, stuffed what clothing he figured he might need into one side and his cooking and eating utensils plus what grub he had in the other. That done, he made up his blanket roll, covered it with his slicker, and returned to the bay.

Attaching the bags and the roll to the saddle, he started to mount up, pleased that it had taken so short a time to ready himself, and then hesitated. Going back into the house, he took a near full box of cartridges for the forty-five he carried on his hip, added them to the other items in his saddlebags, and then rode on into town.

He went first to the town's physician, Masters, told him what had happened to Amos, and asked him to go there at once to attend the old man. He also asked the doctor to recruit someone to stay with Cord until he was in a position to care for himself. Masters gave his word he would do so.

It was growing late in the afternoon by then and he had wanted to be well on his way to Abilene by that hour; he had one more stop to make, however, before he rode out. Angling in to the hitch rack fronting the office of Town Marshal Bert Teasdale,

Medley dismounted and entered the small structure. He found the lawman at his desk going through a stack of wanted posters.

Teasdale looked up as Medley came through the doorway. "Howdy, Tom. What brings you to town?"

"Amos Cord got shot and robbed. Was those two hired hands of his that did it. I'm going after them."

The lawman rose slowly, a frown tearing at his rutted features. "Well, now, maybe you best wait a minute, let the law—"

"No time for that," Tom snapped. "Wasn't only his money they took, but they stole that big copper-dun stallion of his. I've got to catch up with them before they can sell him."

"Damn!" Teasdale murmured. "The old man was right proud of that horse. Expect he's taking it plenty hard. Is he bad hurt?"

"Pretty much. I dropped by Doc Masters and sent him out to fix up Amos. I'll be obliged if you'll stop by his place—and mine, too—whenever you get a chance. I've got Earl Craig's boy looking after things, but it would sure make me feel better if you'd have a look-in."

The marshal nodded. "Be glad to, Tom. . . . Only thing, I ain't so sure your taking the law into your own hands is a good idea. Ought to let—"

"I don't aim to make something big out of it—I'm after the horse, that's all. Doubt if Donner or Trigg will put up any argument."

"Maybe not . . . You know, I never did cotton to that pair. Always figured they was trash, and that sooner or later they'd skin the old man—"

Tom had pivoted and was moving toward the door. Bert Teasdale stepped out from behind his desk.

"Best you watch yourself, Tom," he warned. "Man can't ever tell about jaspers like them."

"I'll be doing just that," Medley replied, and freeing the bay's reins, mounted and rode off down Waggomann's one street.

4

He'd ride until well into the evening, Tom decided, throwing a glance at the sun, now low in the cloud-banked western sky. Donner and Trigg had probably a two-day start on him, so it was important that he try and gain as much time on them as possible.

There was a town on ahead some twenty miles or so—Bear Springs he thought it was called. It would be smart to continue on until he reached it, halt, get a few hours' sleep, and then pull out early in the morning.

The two outlaws would stick to the main road east, Tom believed, but there was no real assurance of that. They could, in an attempt to leave no trace of their passage since they were leading a horse that no man would fail to notice, cut off and do their traveling on one of the less-frequented trails. Amos Cord had figured they'd take no pains to conceal their movements since they thought him dead and therefore unable to pass on any information as to their intentions, but Trigg and Donner just could be cagey enough to take precautions anyway.

Amos ... Medley's thoughts turned to his old friend as the bay loped steadily on through the fading day. He hoped Cord, undoubtedly now in the care of Doc Masters, was resting easy, and on the way to recovery. Tom had never before met anyone like Amos Cord—a kind, friendly man with boundless faith in everyone he encountered regardless of circumstances. Medley had often heard it said of some person that he'd give the shirt off his back as an act of kindness, but Amos Cord was the only man he'd ever encountered where the saying was actually true.

That was what stirred such deep anger within Tom Medley, prompting him to turn his back on his own ranch at a time when his presence there was most necessary. Rufe Donner ... Ike Trigg. Both had been down and out and needing help in the worst way. Amos had taken them in, fed them, and given them a job along with a place to live. The two had returned the favor by trying to kill him and stealing the most important possession the old horse rancher owned—his prized stallion.

Unconsciously Tom Medley swore aloud, the crackling words audible above the rhythmic beat of the bay's hoofs. No matter what it took he'd find the two thieves and recover the stud. In so doing he could partly repay Amos Cord for all he'd done for him.

Abruptly a buck bounded across the road a few yards ahead of Tom, head and tail high, legs stiff. The bay faltered in stride at the deer's sudden appearance and then, recovering, resumed his steady, ground-covering gait.

He could have used the meat the buck would have provided, Tom thought, his eyes following the fleeing deer until it vanished into the brush. As matters stood now he could ill afford to slaughter one of his beeves, and four quarters of venison hanging in his cool shed would have kept him well supplied with steaks and roasts for weeks.

Medley became aware that darkness was closing in and that it had started to rain. Glancing up, he saw that the mass of dark clouds he'd noted earlier on the western horizon were now overhead and rapidly filling the sky with a thick overcast. A wry grin pulled at his mouth. He was in for one of the hard, lashing rainstorms that periodically struck the Mogollon country, he guessed, and without halting the bay gelding, he removed the slicker from his blanket roll and drew it on.

The first furious onslaught of drops hit him just as he broke clear of the mountains and rode out into the plains. The wind-whipped water hammered at him fiercely and in no time at all, despite the raincoat he'd put on, he was soaking wet.

Medley could have turned off into the brush and perhaps found some protection from the gusting storm, but he gave the idea no thought. A single-minded man, he had determined his next stop would be the settlement of Bear Springs, which, he figured, would enable him to trim the lead Ike Trigg and Rufe Donner had over him to some extent, thus he would not halt until he reached there.

Around two hours later, thoroughly wet, in grim humor, Tom Medley rode into Bear Springs, the storm over. He pointed straight for the livery stable which, he recalled from a previous visit, was at the opposite end of the single, narrow street—unless there'd been a change. It was still there, he saw; it appeared there were few other changes in the settlement, although in the darkness of the night the signs above the various business houses, with the exception of the saloons, were not too visible.

A hostler met him in the runway of the stable as he entered. An elderly, bearded man in overalls, undershirt, and thick-soled shoes, he had pulled on a faded, checked mackinaw against the night's damp chill.

"Wet night," he commented as Tom dismounted. "My name's Donovan."

Medley nodded. "Look after him," he said, untying his saddlebags and blanket roll and hanging them across a shoulder. He'd have quite a bit of drying out to do once he got in a hotel room. "Be leaving for Abilene early in the morning."

The stableman nodded. "Sure—I'll have him ready. Cost you an extra four bits, but I'll rub him down good if you want. Got a line in the back where I can dry out that blanket, too."

Medley said, "Fine," and handed over the sodden woolen cover. "Give the bay all the grain he wants—"

"Sure enough," Donovan said, and then added with a grin, "I misdoubt he'll be needing much water, however."

The humor was lost on Medley. Near the last of the stalls at the end of the runway a woman had appeared. She quickly crossed over and entered a room in the back of the musty, malodorous structure. Donovan's wife, Tom supposed, turning his attention again to the stableman.

"You see anything of two men riding through here in the last couple of days? They would have been leading a big copper-dun stud."

Donovan, hand on the bay's headstall as he prepared to lead the horse off to a stall, thought for a moment, and then wagged his head.

"Nope, don't recollect no such fellows with an animal like that."

That Donner and Trigg could have bypassed the settlement came as no great surprise to Tom. The outlaws had left Amos Cord's ranch during the early hours of the day and would have no reason to stop in Bear Springs. Of course they could have halted outside the town and left the stud while they spent an hour or two in one of the saloons, but most likely they had simply swung wide and kept going until dark.

"Have my horse ready by first light," Medley said then, and coming about, he returned to the street and bent his steps toward the town's liveliest saloon, the Painted Lady, which also rented rooms.

It was not too crowded, being that time of week when most cowhands and miners were kept to their jobs, but there were a dozen or so men scattered about, some at the bar, a few at the tables playing cards, others just lounging about either standing or sitting in chairs tipped back against the rough plank wall.

The piano player was at his instrument, but at the moment, drink in hand, he was in conversation with one of several gaudily dressed girls lazing about. The heavy smell of smoke, liquor, sweat, perfume, coal oil, and his own wet clothing was strong in Medley's nostrils as he crossed the room. He was aware, too, of the abrupt cessation of talk as he shouldered his way through the swinging doors and entered the saloon, and then its resumption a few moments later when, curiosity satisfied, the Painted Lady's customers returned to whatever had been occupying them.

Taking his place among the men at the counter, Tom ordered a glass of whiskey from the bartender, a moon-faced man wearing, among other odd bits of clothing, a checked vest. When the shot of liquor came, Medley laid a silver dollar on the bar, downed the whiskey, and nodded to the man behind the counter.

"Any chance of getting a bite to eat? And I'll be needing a room for the night—"

Wordless, the bartender reached under the counter and produced a plate of sliced beef and cold biscuits.

"All we've got's this," he said, and then jerked a thumb toward a cloudy-looking jar at the end of the bar. "Pickled eggs, if you want some."

It was a hell of a poor meal for a man who'd not only been in the saddle for several hours but had weathered a rainstorm as well—but it would have to do. Tom shrugged.

"Give me another drink," he said, helping himself to the meat and biscuits that he piled onto a tin plate the bartender had provided. "How much more do I owe you—including a room?"

"Make it two dollars—"

Tom handed over the specified amount and turned to one of the unoccupied tables. The bartender's voice followed him.

"Take any of them rooms upstairs. They're all empty."

Medley made no reply, and sitting down at the table with his food and drink, began to eat. Immediately one of the girls separated from a group of several cowhands and sauntered up to him.

"You're just what I've been waiting for," she said, smiling. "I'm Adelina."

Tom, in no mood for frivolity of any kind, glanced up. Adelina was a dark-eyed, dark-haired, well-built woman with what was popularly termed an hourglass figure. Clad in a short, low-cut yel-low dress, her brown skin contrasted sharply.

Medley shook his head. "Move on," he said gruffly.

Adelina didn't stir. "You got something against women?"

Tom paused in his eating. "Nope," he replied irritably, and then softening his tone, added, "You'd look mighty tempting to me if I wasn't so damn beat and didn't have things on my mind."

The girl's smile widened. "Maybe I could sort of help—make you forget—"

"No!" Medley snapped, suddenly out of patience. "Get the hell away from here and let me eat."

At Tom's lifted voice several men standing nearby came about. One, features flushed, eyes bright, frowned and crossed unsteadily to Medley's table.

"Who you yelling at?" he demanded thickly. "This here little girl's a special friend of mine, and—"

"I don't give a damn who or what she is!" Tom shot back, weariness and frustration surging through him. "I just aim—"

"Well, you ain't talking to her or me neither that away!" the drunk shouted, and lunging forward, seized Medley by the lapels of his slicker and jerked him out of his chair.

"Fight!" someone nearby yelled, and immedi-ately everyone in the saloon surged toward Med-ley and the drunk.

"Get him, Junior!" another voice shouted. "Show him how the cow ate the cabbage!"

Medley brought up his arms, broke Junior's grip on the slicker. The man was very drunk, Tom realized then, and in no condition to fight—something he, personally, was in no mood for either.

"Get the hell away from me!" Medley snarled, and placing the flat of his hands against Junior's chest, gave the drunk a hard shove and sent him staggering back into the onlookers.

More shouts filled the Painted Lady. Ignoring them, Tom settled back down to finish his meal. What little whiskey there was in his glass had been spilled when Junior jarred the table, but he ignored the lack; he'd get a refill when he was finished eating.

"You're plenty mean when it comes to pushing drunks around," a voice said from behind him. "Maybe you'd like to try your luck with me."

Medley, anger and exasperation rising again within him, put the last bit of meat in his mouth, chewed briefly, and swallowed. Then, without looking around, he rose suddenly from his chair. Fist knotted into an iron-hard ball, he pivoted and swung at the dark, bearded face glaring at him. The blow caught the man flush on the jaw. He rocked to one side, head wobbling loosely, fell back against the wall, and collapsed into a heap on the floor.

Medley's reaction had been so swift and unexpected that others in the saloon stood in startled silence for several moments, and then, as Tom took up his empty glass and moved to the bar, the

38

hush broke. There was a rush of talk, laughter, and two or three of the men slapped Medley on the shoulder.

Acknowledging it all with a slight nod of his head, Tom motioned to the bartender for another drink.

"I'll have one more," he said quietly, laying the necessary coin on the counter. Downing the liquor, he slung his saddlebags over a shoulder and crossed to the stairway.

"He's sure a tough son of a bitch, ain't he?"

At the comment Medley, about a third of the way up the stairs, halted. The urge to turn, go back down the steps, and take to task the man who had uttered the slurring remark swept through him. But a moment later weariness from the day's work, the long ride to Bear Springs, the battering from the storm, all coupled with the realization of what lay ahead for him, took over. Shrugging indifferently, he continued on up to the saloon's second floor.

5

A hallway led directly off the balcony-like landing, and remembering the bartender's words to the effect that all the rooms were empty, Tom crossed to the first door on his right, opened it, and entered the dark, stuffy room beyond.

Pausing to strike a match, Medley located a bracketed lamp on the wall adjacent to the entrance and, raising the chimney, turned up the wick and lit it. As mellow light flooded the small, cheerless cubicle, furnished only with bed, a scarred chair, wardrobe, and combination dresser and washstand, he closed the door, turned the key.

Coming about, he crossed to the single window in the opposite wall. Raising it, he felt the rush of cool air on his face and for a long breath stood motionless enjoying its freshness. Then, wheeling, he began to remove his damp clothing.

He had gotten wet to the skin, and peeling off everything from the slicker down, he dried himself with a flour-sack towel that hung from the washstand, and then drew on the extra pair of clean drawers he'd put in his saddlebags. Medley felt much better after that, wished now that he'd bought a bottle of whiskey while he had been at the bar; a drink would ease the tension that still gripped him.

But he reckoned he could do without. To get a bottle meant putting on his damp clothing again and going downstairs; it simply wasn't all that important. Yawning, Tom blew out the lamp, turned to the bed, and sat down, vaguely aware of the piano music and rumble of noise coming from below and the dry rustle of the bed's cornhusk mattress as he stretched out full length.

Medley had barely closed his eyes when he heard a knock on the door. Anger surfaced instantly once more. It was either one or more of Adelina's friends anxious to pursue what Junior and his dark, bearded sidekick had started, or it was the woman herself.

"Get the hell away from there!" he shouted.

A few moments of silence followed his harsh command, and then the knock sounded again—this time accompanied by a woman's urgent voice.

"Please—let me in. Please!"

It didn't sound like the saloon girl Adelina. There was a slight accent—Spanish, he thought—to her words. Tom remained where he lay, his tired brain weighing the possibilities of a ruse being staged by Junior's or maybe Adelina's friends; or maybe it

41

was just another of the Painted Lady's women a bit more enterprising than the others.

"Please let me in! I—I have to talk to you."

Medley got to his feet, reached for his pants, hung across a chair's back to dry, and pulled them on. Drawing his pistol from the holster hanging from a bedpost, he crossed to the door, released the lock, and turned the knob. In the half-dark of the hallway he had a glimpse of a woman's strained, taut features before him, and then in the next brief lapse of a second or two she had slipped by him and was in the room.

"Damn it to hell," Medley exploded, pivoting, "what—"

"Just listen to me—please!" the young woman said, her voice coming from a far corner of the room. "Can you light a lamp?"

Tom dug into a pocket of his oilskin pack of matches, struck one, and lit the wall lamp again. As its glow filled the room, he put his angry, frowning glance on the girl.

She wasn't very old, he saw—probably eighteen, certainly twenty at the most. Dressed in a man's clothing, she had a wealth of dark hair, but it had been gathered onto the top of her head and a worn and stained gray hat had been pulled over it. Her eyes showed blue in the soft light, and the loosely fitting man's shirt, jacket, and pants did little to conceal her well-turned body. She was pretty, but there was a sort of determined set to her mouth and chin that bespoke strength and independence.

"Now what's this all about?" Medley demanded.

He'd seen good-looking women before in his drifting about the country, most of whom it seemed had problems, and this occasion appeared to be no different from any of them. Best thing to do was hear her out, explain there was nothing he could do, and send her on her way so that he might get some sleep. First light came mighty early.

"I need help, your help," the girl said, moving up to the bed and sitting on its edge. "My name's Lucilla—Lucilla Kinkaid. I don't think I heard anyone downstairs mention your name, only that you were a—"

Medley grinned in spite of himself. He hadn't told it, he thought, and the woman had heard only what some man in the crowd had termed him. "It's Tom Medley."

"Can I stay here with you tonight?" Lucilla continued as he crossed slowly and sank into a chair. "There's some men—three of them—after me. They'll kill me if they find me."

"Why?" Tom asked skeptically.

"I—I saw them do something—kill a man, in fact, and rob a place. They're afraid I'll tell the law."

"Why don't you? That'd be the thing to do."

Lucilla Kinkaid shook her head and looked down. Her profile was nicely formed; it reminded Medley of the face on a delicately carved cameo that he had seen somewhere during his wandering.

"I can't—at least not yet. Besides, I was sort of mixed up in it."

Tom considered her narrowly. What she had just said was hard to believe. Lucilla didn't look like the sort of girl who would be the member of a gang of killers and thieves.

"I didn't know what they—the men I was with—were up to. I was just along with them, and then when they killed that man—he was a lawman of some kind—I ran off, ran away from them. They've been hunting for me ever since."

"How long is that?"

"A week now, more or less—"

"Where'd it happen?"

"Arizona, I think, or it could have been in New Mexico. Town's called Cutterville, or Carterville, I'm not sure which. Anyway, it was right on the border . . . It be all right if I stay here tonight with you? They'd never think of looking for me in your room."

Medley shrugged. "Reckon so. It'll be up to you where you sleep—I'll be on the bed. What happens in the morning? I've got to ride out early."

Lucilla pursed her lips in deep thought. "Which direction?"

"East—for Abilene."

The girl nodded hurriedly. "That would be fine for me, I'm trying to get to some folks—relations in Fort Worth where I'll be safe. I think it's on past Abilene, isn't it?"

Tom swore silently. "You asking to ride with me to Abilene?"

"If you'll let me! I won't get in your way and I won't hold you back," Lucilla said earnestly, her features anxious. "I've a good horse, and I can ride better than most men."

Abilene was a long way from Bear Springs, Medley reminded himself, and he wasn't interested in having company. Such always complicated things, it seemed, and in this particular situation—a girl with three outlaw partners after her—he'd like as not get himself sucked into the worst kind of trouble. As well be blunt about it, tell her no.

"Got problems of my own," he began. "Friend of mine got shot, and—" He broke off. Why go into it? It should be enough just to say that he had important matters of his own to attend to.

He glanced at Lucilla, prepared to tell her in so many plain words that accompanying him was out of the question, but the face turned to him was so youthful, so hopeful that resolution weakened.

"We'll talk about it in the morning," he said. "I'm dead on my feet—need sleep."

Rising, he walked the short width of the room to the lamp, extinguished it, and then dropping back to the bed, he thrust his pistol under his pillow and stretched out. He felt the girl rise and move to the chair, saying nothing. It was her choice, Tom thought; Lucilla could lie down beside him

45

and be perfectly safe insofar as he was concerned, but if she preferred to sit up the remainder of the night, it was all right with him.

Medley awoke a few minutes before first light, some inner timepiece arousing him at the proper, planned-for time. Immediately he became aware that he was not on the bed alone, and turning slowly, he saw the girl, still fully clothed, lying beside him.

A stir of sympathy moved through Tom. Lucilla looked so young and innocent, her smooth, lightly tanned features so soft and womanly. How could she have gotten herself involved with a bunch of outlaws?

Abruptly Lucilla's eyes opened. They spread with alarm, and she sat up quickly.

Medley shrugged and, swinging his legs off the bed, got to his feet. "Expect we'd best get started," he heard himself say, and frowned as he sat down in the chair to put on his boots. The words had come without conscious thought, but now that he had voiced them, he felt pleased. Lucilla needed help—needed him, in fact—and when it got right down to rock bottom, there was no good reason why he shouldn't give her a hand.

Lucilla had come off the bed instantly. A smile parted her lips. "You mean that you'll let me ride with you?"

"You're welcome to come along far as I go. Maybe to Abilene, could be somewheres this side."

She hurried around to where his shirt was hanging from a peg in the wall, and shaking it vigorously, she handed it to him. "This is still damp," she commented, and then added, "It won't matter if you don't go all the way to Abilene—I'll manage the rest of the way somehow. Just to get out of this part of the country and over into Texas is all I ask."

"Understood you to say you wanted to go to some kin of yours—in Fort Worth, I think it was," Medley said, putting on the shirt.

"Oh, I do! I meant that if I can ride with you just halfway it will help that much. They—the men who are after me—won't expect me to be with somebody, and like as not, even if they should see us, they won't think it's me, only that it's some man and woman going somewhere."

"Don't they know the kind of horse you're riding?"

It was steadily growing lighter, and now Lucilla Kinkaid's features were more definite. "I suppose so. If you think it best, I could swap my buckskin for something else. I could make a deal with that stableman, probably."

"It might be a good idea," Tom agreed. "You ready?" he continued, hanging the saddlebags over a shoulder.

She nodded and moved to the door. Unlocking it, she looked out into the hall, carefully checking both directions. Satisfied all was clear, the girl then completed her exit, hesitating again as she pointed to the far end of the corridor.

"There's a back way," she said.

"Fine with me," Medley replied, not sure if Lucilla feared being seen by the men following her if she went out the front, or was reluctant for anyone present in the saloon downstairs to know that she had spent the night in his room.

They reached the stable without incident. Donovan had Medley's bay saddled and ready to go. The wool blanket the stableman had taken charge of was now dry and awaited only Tom's slicker to be rolled and put in its customary place. Donovan had also prepared a small sack of grain, which he'd tied onto the saddle.

"Figured you'd best be carrying a little feed for the gelding," he said, pointing to the sack. "Cost you another two-bits on top of what you owe me."

Tom reached into his pocket for some change. "How much altogether?"

"Couple of dollars'll cover it—"

Medley handed over the amount specified for the bay's care and began to make up his blanket roll. Lucilla had gone on down the runway and was saddling her mount. Evidently she had decided to keep the horse she was riding, a buckskin, she'd said. Tom guessed it didn't really matter; at a distance the color of a horse was pretty indefinite. Such was especially true of a buckskin.

Blanket roll in place, Medley swung up into the saddle and put his attention on the girl. She had come out of one of the back stalls and entered the runway. There was something familiar to it—to the way she walked and looked. Tom suddenly remembered. She had been in the stable that night before when he rode in. Undoubtedly she had heard him tell Donovan that he would be heading out for Abilene that next morning.

Lucilla had known all along that he was going to Abilene when she came to his room in the Painted Lady. Why hadn't she come right out and said so, instead of acting as if she was unaware of the fact?

"I'm all ready," Tom heard the woman say, and looking around, he saw that she was beside him on the buckskin.

He nodded brusquely. "We'll do our eating later on the trail," he said curtly, and touching the bay with his spurs, he headed him out into the brightening day.

6

The road followed a gradually descending slope out into the plains, and by the time they were well onto the flat, the first signs of sunrise were making themselves visible beyond the ragged rim of the San Andres hills far to the east.

"It's beautiful—"

Tom Medley glanced at Lucilla. She was to his left, her buckskin mare almost shoulder to shoulder with the bay. It was the first either of them had spoken since they'd ridden out of Bear Springs, and the sound of her voice surprised him.

"Yeh—the sun coming up," he said, looking to the east.

Long streaks of salmon, red, and yellow lay parallel to the ragged horizon, while fanning high above them was an embankment of glistening pearl. Tom had been aware of sunsets, and their counterparts, sunrises, as far back as he could recall, and although impressed on occasion by their brilliance, he, like most other men, had simply taken them for granted. Now, through the eyes of someone else he was having his appreciation of the phenomenon.

"Sure is," he agreed, coming back to Lucilla's remark. "Just never paid much attention before."

The eastern sky had changed swiftly. The salmon had faded into the yellow, and now darker shades of red were spraying into the pearl background. But even as they watched while the horses loped steadily on, the reds disappeared and the arch above the horizon became a wall of shining yellow pierced by shafts of gold. And then suddenly the sun was there. A small, curving bit of purest white at first, it grew quickly into a blinding orb, forcing both Lucilla and Medley to tip their hats forward and shade their eyes from its glare.

A warmness began to spread over the land, dispelling the night's chill. Birds were moving about—horned larks that sprang vertically into the sky from the scrub grass and weeds, doves that deserted the larger clumps of rabbitbrush and whirred erratically off into the morning, and high overhead a pair of hunting hawks were soaring lazily against the steel blue of the sky. Off to the left of the trail a gopher appeared, ran for a short distance, and then, standing erect, voiced a shrill challenge to the passing riders.

"Spring on ahead a couple of miles," Tom said. "We'll pull up there, fix ourselves a bite to eat."

Lucilla nodded. "Sounds like you've been across here before."

"Once, maybe twice," Medley replied.

There were few places of note in the frontier west that he hadn't been during the course of his drifting, he realized, but a man usually alone and accustomed to his own company and silence, he made no mention of the fact.

"You live somewhere around that town—Bear Springs?" the girl asked.

"No. Got a place back up in the Mogollon country. Ain't much yet—but I'm working at it."

"You married?"

Tom shook his head. "Never have had anything to offer a woman."

Lucilla was quiet for a long minute. Then, "Did you ever come right down to asking a woman to marry you?"

"No—"

"Maybe you should have—you might've been surprised at the answer you got. Most women are a lot stronger than men think, and there are plenty who don't care a hoot about having a fancy home and all the fixings—not if they're in love with the man."

Medley made no reply. He knew a bit about the subject—far too much, in fact—but he was in no mood to discuss it.

"Those trees up ahead, to the south—that's where the spring is. We'll stop there—but not for long. Got to keep moving."

Lucilla frowned slightly, apparently wondering just why Tom Medley was in such a hurry, but she voiced no question; when they drew up under the cluster of cottonwoods, now well leafed out after the starkness of winter, she immediately took over the chore of preparing a meal from Medley's stock of trail grub.

There wasn't much of it, and only the bare minimum of necessities to work with—a frying pan, a tin that he used for brewing coffee, a solitary cup, plate, fork, and spoon.

"Wasn't expecting company," he explained, taking the canteens off the saddles so that they could be refilled with fresh water from the spring. "Next town we come to I'll pick up another cup and plate, and such."

"You need some groceries, too," Lucilla said, considering the small supply disapprovingly. "Hardly enough here for one meal—and not exactly the sort of—"

"I'll stock up on grub, too," he cut in. "Like I said, I wasn't figuring on having a partner on the trail with me, and aimed to travel fast and light."

Lucilla made no further comment but set about getting together a breakfast from the stock of food she'd found in his saddlebags. Tom built a small, hot fire, and while she worked at making coffee and frying up some of the salt pork and warming the hard bread, he watered the horses and picketed them on the young grass growing along the banks of the spring. Later, as they sat in the bright sunshine enjoying the last of Lucilla's coffee, she turned to him.

"You seem to be in a big hurry to reach Abilene. Why? Does it have something to do with that friend of yours that you said was shot?"

Tom nodded. "I'm paying off a favor."

Lucilla looked at him blankly. "A favor? I don't understand—"

"Friend of mine, Amos Cord, back in the Mogollon country—I owe him my life. He's an old man, raises horses. Picked me up on the trail one day. Was all shot up—dying. He took me to his cabin, doctored me up. I would've thrown in my hand if it hadn't been for him." Tom hesitated, dug into a shirt pocket for cigarette makings, found none. That was something else he'd buy when he laid in a stock of grub.

"You know, to this day he's never asked me how I come to be laying there alongside the trail bleeding to death."

"If he's the one you're doing the favor for, I can understand why," Lucilla murmured.

"He's the one. A few days ago the two hired hands that worked for him—he took them in, too, gave them jobs and a place to live when they showed up flat busted and hungry—jumped him. They shot him in the back, then beat and robbed him. On top of that they stole the horse he'd all but starved to buy and raise—a fine, copper-dun stud."

"Copper dun?" Lucilla repeated. "I don't think I've ever seen a horse that color."

"You don't come across them too often, especially one like this one of Amos'. To me a horse has always just been something to ride—a way to get me from here to yonder and back without walking—but that stud, I sure have to admit he's one hell of a horse.

"Stood a good fifteen, maybe sixteen hands high, and I expect he'll go a thousand pounds. Heard Amos brag about him having perfect conformation, which I reckon means he was built just right. He's got black hooves, and black around the eyes, which is a good thing in this country, and there's not a hair on him, except around his eyes, that ain't copper-dun color."

"Copper dun," Lucilla said thoughtfully, "I guess that's a sort of sorrel—"

"A little, but I figure it more a light chestnut with something in it that gives it a darker, off shade. Some folks call it bronze. He's probably the handsomest horse I've ever seen. Even the thoroughbreds I've come across along the Mississippi don't show up as good as he does.

"Amos had big plans for the stud. He'd brought in some good chestnut mares, aimed to breed them this summer and fall when their time come. The stud's about three years old, so Amos was looking forward to a fine bunch of colts late next winter and spring."

"So you took it on yourself to go after your friend's horse, get it back for him."

Tom glanced at the girl, and then, tipping the tin of coffee to his lips, he finished its contents. He felt a bit self-conscious. He'd done a lot of talking—something unusual for him—and was now somewhat embarrassed by it.

"Yes, what I aim to do. Horse means a lot to Amos," he said.

"What makes you so sure that the two men headed for Abilene?"

"Amos heard them say that's where they'd take the stud. They figured he was dead—or dying, but he fooled them. I happened by a day or two later, not sure which, and he was still alive. Got the doctor for him. Expect he's coming along all right now."

"He must be a tough old man," Lucilla commented, beginning to collect the utensils used for the meal. "If you had the law telegraph the sheriff or marshal—whatever they've got there—he ought to have the two horse thieves locked up and waiting for you. Means you don't have to hurry all that much."

Tom Medley lifted his head in surprise. He hadn't thought of that! He could have told Bert Teasdale there in Waggomann to get word to the telegraph office in Silver City, ask them to pass it on to Abilene, but it hadn't occurred to him. Hell, he hadn't even told Teasdale that he was heading for Abilene, only that he was going after Donner and Trigg. But maybe he'd get lucky; maybe Amos Cord would mention Abilene to the marshal and ask if he'd sent a telegram to the lawman there about the thieves.

"Something I didn't do," he said then, rising and helping the woman load up. "Just slipped my mind."

Lucilla smiled. "Not hard to understand that. You're a man used to doing everything yourself. Never occurs to you to ask help from somebody else."

He shook his head. "Was a fool thing to forget—"

"I doubt if it will make any difference," Lucilla said, pausing to look at several scrub jays noisily flitting about in a nearby cottonwood. "What were they going to do with the horse when they got there?"

"One of them, Donner I think it was, said he knew a rancher who'd pay a lot of money—a thousand dollars—for him."

"We shouldn't have any trouble finding them there then," the girl said, preparing to mount.

Tom Medley glanced at Lucilla, aware of the pronoun she had used. He swung up into his saddle and cut the bay about.

"I don't want to mix you up in this—keep you from going on to see your kin," he said. "If it comes down to gunplay, that'll bring in the law, and the law could tie things up for days."

"Oh, I didn't mean it that way, exactly," Lucilla hastened to explain. "I only meant that, well, that's

57

where the two horse thieves will be if they have a buyer who'll pay a big price for the copper dun."

Tom remained silent as the girl, now aboard the buckskin, clucked the little mare into forward motion. When she had passed by, he dropped in behind and then drew the bay abreast. Medley was wondering again about her, about Fort Worth, and the relatives there she intended to visit and seek safety with. Was there any truth to any of it?

7

Around noon they reached the Rio Grande, found it running high, thanks to the spring rains. They spent a full hour finding a place to ford the swirling, muddy current, but finally across, they angled back to the road east and once again continued the journey to Abilene.

A short time later they came to a small Mexican village where Tom was able to purchase supplies from a general merchandise store run by a man named Solomon. During the course of conversation Medley asked the merchant if he had noticed the passing by of two men leading a fine, copper-dun horse. Solomon agreed at once that he had.

"When?" Tom wanted to know.

The merchant gave that brief consideration and then bobbed his head. "Yes," he said positively, "it was yesterday morning. The sun was not long up."

Medley felt a surge of satisfaction. Donner and Trigg were only a day and a half ahead of him.

With luck and no unexpected trouble or delay he should be able to overtake the pair well this side of Abilene.

"They act like they was in a hurry?"

Solomon again gave the question his full attention. Finally he shook his head. "No, I would not say so. They stand around and talk, drinking from the bottle of whiskey they buy from me. . . . It was a fine animal they had, all right—one I felt did not belong to them—"

The merchant let his comment hang as if expecting some sort of answer, a statement perhaps to the effect that the horse had been stolen. Medley, collecting his purchases, only shrugged.

"Much obliged," he said, and returned to the hitch rack fronting the store.

Tying the flour sack filled with the articles purchased from Solomon to the saddle horn, Medley mounted the bay and rode out, once more following the road that led due east. It would not be wise, they had both agreed, for Lucilla to show herself at the store. The men searching for her, should they pick up her trail, would certainly halt at Solomon's and ask the merchant if she had passed that way. A negative answer from Solomon could throw them off.

Lucilla was waiting for him in a grove of trees a short distance on ahead. When he rejoined her, she was off her saddle taking it easy in the cool shade while the buckskin cropped at the short grass growing nearby. When she saw Medley approaching, she rose quickly to meet him and smiled at sight of the well-filled flour sack.

"Now I can fix us some decent meals—not just fried salt pork and grease bread! Were you able to get everything?"

"Everything you named off—and a bit more," Tom replied, tapping the shirt pocket where he now carried tobacco and papers for cigarettes. He also had replaced the bottle of whiskey customarily carried in his saddlebags, but he didn't think it necessary to tell her of that.

He watched as the girl caught up the buckskin, mounted, and came alongside him. Then, "Found out Donner and Trigg were by here yesterday morning," he said as they moved out. "Not in any big hurry, according to the fellow who runs that store."

"Do you think we might catch up with them?" Lucilla asked, raising her voice to be heard above the clatter of the horses' hooves as they crossed a flinty knoll in the road.

"Good chance if somebody don't slow us down."

The girl glanced at him. "Somebody? You mean the men I told you about—that are after me?"

Medley drew out of his sack of tobacco and sheaf of papers and began to roll a cigarette. They were off the rocky area now and back in the ankle-deep dust.

"About the only people I can think of that's hunting us."

Lucilla shrugged. "I'm sorry if I'm getting in the

way of what you have to do. When I talked to you last night in your room I didn't know why you were going to Abilene—only that you were."

"And that wasn't any surprise to you either, was it? You'd heard me tell Donovan there in the livery stable that I'd be headed out that way the next morning."

Lucilla's eyes reflected her surprise. Again her shoulders stirred. "I didn't mean it to be a lie. I just let you think that—"

"Probably a few more things that you're sort of hiding from me, I expect. I'll take it as a favor if you'll let me know what I'm up against."

There was no anger in Tom Medley's voice, only a quiet insistence that said plainly he wanted a full explanation of the situation he'd more or less allowed her to sucker him into.

"Can start with the bottom card in the deck— are there for sure three men trailing you? I need an honest answer."

"I'll give you one," Lucilla said, coming up straight in the saddle and facing him squarely. "Yes, there are—they were not far behind me when I got to Bear Springs. A half-day, maybe less."

"Can be sure they picked up our trail there," Tom said, his tone softening a bit. "First man they'd ask about you would be Donovan at the livery stable, and he'd have no reason for not telling them which way you—we'd gone."

"I suppose," Lucilla replied wearily. "It seems

like I've been on the run for months—hiding, worrying—"

"Now's the time to tell me why," Medley cut in bluntly.

Lucilla was staring straight ahead at the low-lying mass of smooth mountains not too far in the distance. She nodded.

"Only right you know—you were kind enough to let me come along with you." The girl paused, looked back over a shoulder as if to assure herself they were not being followed. Satisfied no riders were in sight, she resumed her contemplation of the hills. "I'd hoped that leaving with you would throw Sid and the others off—still do, in fact, but maybe—"

"Sid—he one of them?"

"Yes, my stepbrother. My pa died when I was small, little more than a baby. Ma then married a man named Hazelwood. He had three sons of his own—Sid's one of them. Then Ma and him had three children. Sid's brothers made it real rough for me after we grew up, and I kept looking for a chance to run away. Sid wasn't as bad as Emil and Josh, so when he come up with the idea of me joining in with him and a couple of his friends and going to Dodge City, I was all for it. I figured I could get a job of some kind there—anything would be better than fighting off Emil and Josh two or three times a week.

"What I didn't know was that Sid and his friends, John Payton and Red Mescole—both outlaws—were planning to hold up a bank. By the time I found out about it, it was too late—I think I told you all this back in your room. Anyway, as soon as I could, I got away. It was all strange country to me, of course, and I didn't know exactly where to go. I just kept riding and finally ended up in Bear Springs."

"And you figure they're out to shut you up—"

Lucilla nodded slowly. Her eyes were still fixed on the formations to the east. From the side her face appeared to Medley as if it had been carved from some soft, delicate substance.

"Maybe they won't pick up our trail right away," he said, a sort of resignation in his voice. "Can hope for that, anyway."

"But if they do, then what?" Her words were barely audible above the thud of the loping horses.

Tom shifted his attention to the girl, found her studying him, features still, eyes dark and troubled. There was anxiety in her manner.

"We'll do what we can to lose them. I know this country pretty good. Chance they don't."

The reply seemed to satisfy Lucilla, and she turned her gaze again to the road ahead. "I hope we can," she said after a time. "I don't want you to have to fight them—three of them—shoot it out. It wouldn't be fair—and it's not really your problem—"

"Won't come down to that if I can help it," Tom said. "I've got a chore of my own to see to—one that may call for gunplay, so I can do without mixing it up with your three friends."

"They're far from being friends, or anything else," Lucilla said ruefully. Then, "Would you like for me to leave, go on to Abilene by myself? There doesn't appear to be anyone following, and if I stay on this road—"

"No, we headed out together so we'll stay that way. I'll see you clear to Abilene; after that, you're on your own."

"I'll manage—and I'm grateful to you for what you've already done, and are doing," Lucilla said, and fell silent.

They rode on through the warm, crystal-clear day, halting at noon by a lone juniper to have a cold lunch while the horses rested; then they pushed on for the mountains, now gradually looming larger as they cut down the separating distance. Several times along the way Tom Medley glanced back over the road they had covered. Lucilla, too, continually watched; and neither saw anything until near sundown, when they both caught sight of dust, which a short time later proved to be three riders coming on fast.

They were only small, dark objects in the fading light at first, and there was no way of knowing definitely that it would be Sid Hazelwood and his two friends, but in Medley's mind there was certainty; it could hardly be anyone else, he reasoned. Lucilla agreed with his logic.

"What can we do?" she asked.

There was no fear in her voice, no panic in her manner. It was simply a question as to what course they should take.

"Go on till dark," Tom said, gauging the distance remaining to the mountains. "Soon as it gets to where they can't see us, we'll cut off the road, head north, and hope they keep going east."

Lucilla silently signified her understanding, and they rode on, now pressing their tired horses for more speed. It was full dark when they reached the first outcropping of the ragged mountains and Tom, throwing a look back to the west and unable to see the riders, immediately swung left off the road and began to follow a narrow trail that paralleled the base of the formation.

Well into the night, with the horses lagging badly and both he and the girl weary of their saddles, Medley pulled to a halt in a deep arroyo and made camp. They ate a cold supper, avoiding a fire, fearing the glow from it might be seen by the outlaws.

"I'll stand watch," Tom said, motioning for the girl to lay out her blanket.

He was tired, impatient, even angry at himself for getting involved in Lucilla Kinkaid's problems. It was already causing him to lose time—and that was something he felt he couldn't afford. If Rufe Donner and Ike Trigg, upon reaching Abilene, were unable to sell the copper-dun stud as planned, they'd move on, and just which direction they took might be difficult to determine. But he was involved;

he had committed himself to seeing the girl safely through to the Texas settlement, and that's what he'd do.

The outlaws apparently fell for the trick, there being no sign of them when morning came. Tom built a small, smokeless fire with dry wood found under a close-by ledge, and Lucilla prepared a breakfast of bacon, corn cakes, and coffee, taking advantage of the opportunity to put several small potatoes in the ashes to bake for future use. The meal over, they were mounted and on their way not long after sunrise, doubling back over the trail they had followed that day before.

"There a pass where we can cut through the mountains on about ten miles or so," Medley said when the girl's questioning glance called for an explanation. "It'll save us a little time."

"What about Sid and the others? Won't they be—"

"Little hard to figure where they'll be," Tom replied a bit gruffly. "Just got to gamble on none of them knowing about the place."

They reached the cut in a little more than an hour, Medley finding it with no difficulty. Climbing the steep slope of the mountain and descending the east side was not done so easily, however, and it was late in the afternoon when Tom called a halt at the foot of the ragged formation.

They could have continued on for another hour or two, as it was far from dark, but Medley, despite the need to hurry on and make up lost time, chose to halt for night camp well ahead of usual. The horses were all in from traveling the difficult, broken trail across the mountain and it was best they stop early and give them a good night's rest.

It would be another dry camp, and they would have to share water with the bay and the buckskin, but that posed no serious problem. They'd be coming to a creek or a spring before the end of the next day.

Well-shielded by a cleft in a butte that thrust out from the foot of the mountain, Tom built a fire and did what he could for the horses while Lucilla got a simple, but satisfying meal together. Few words passed between them while they ate, and when they had finished both, dog tired, they sought their blankets.

"I'm sorry, Tom," Medley heard the girl say as he was drifting off to sleep.

Raising his head, he said, "For what?"

"Sid and the others—they've cost you most of a day."

Tom settled back. "No point fretting about it now. What's done's done. Tomorrow maybe we can gain a little. The country's mostly flats. Won't be so hard traveling."

He had barely closed his eyes after that, it seemed to Medley, when it became time to rise and prepare to move out. Putting a fire together for Lucilla while she got a meal under way, he tightened the saddle cinches of the horses and slipped their bits into place. The sky was a bit cloudy and it appeared they would have a pleasant cool day.

"Ought to make good time," Tom said, turning about to face Lucilla. "Horses had a good rest and—"

The rest of the words he intended to speak died in his throat. Three men, guns drawn, were standing at the edge of the camp.

8

Medley drew up slowly, anger and frustration rolling through him. At that moment Lucilla looked around and had her first glimpse of the outlaws. Her features blanched with alarm, and then she, too, came erect.

"Howdy, little sister," one of the men drawled as together all sauntered with indolent, studied indifference toward the center of the camp.

This would be Sid Hazelwood, the stepbrother, Tom realized. About thirty, he had small, dark eyes, a sandy complexion, a stubble of beard, and a thin, scraggily mustache. He was dressed in faded denims, leather vest, stained gray shirt, high crowned hat, and wore his pistol well forward around his waist.

Tom made a quick assessment of the other two. Red Mescole was easy to identify by the brick-colored hair pushing out under the flat-crowned hat he was wearing. Squat, dark pants filthy with grease and dust, checked shirt open down the front to expose a mass of reddish hair, he had a wide grin on his ruddy face.

Payton would be the third man. Tall, older than his partners, dark eyes set close together, bearded, a full mustache, he had a quiet deadly way about him. Clad in a worn gray suit, faded red shirt, and dark hat, he probably was the most dangerous of the trio.

"You sure pulled a mean trick on us, girl," Hazelwood said, his friendly manner vanishing. "When we get done with this, you got a good beating coming."

"Done with what?" Medley asked coolly.

"Now, best you keep out of something that ain't none of your put in," John Payton warned in a low voice. "This here's between her and us."

"Maybe you think so," Tom countered, "but I got cut in on this game, whatever it is, and I aim to find out what it's all about."

"The hell you say!" Sid Hazelwood snapped. "You ain't in no position to go wanting anything. I'll tell you this much, this damn little biddy went and—"

"Can leave off that," Medley cut in. "She's a lady far as I'm concerned, and I won't stand for no badmouthing."

"By God, you'll stand for whatever we aim to dish out!" Mescole shouted angrily. "You done already caused us a lot of trouble, and I reckon right now's the time we paid you off for doing it."

71

Tom saw the husky redhead's gun come up and made a grab for his own weapon. Both exploded in the same instant. Tom heard Lucilla scream, felt a bullet burn into the upper part of his arm, but he saw Mescole jolt and stagger back a step as a red stain spread across his chest. Abruptly the outlaw sank to the sandy ground.

"The son of a bitch!" Payton yelled. "He's gone and killed Red!"

In the next fragment of time the tall outlaw drew and fired his pistol. Tom, off balance from Mescole's bullet, was unable to react. He flinched, fell back as Payton's bullet seared along the side of his head. Vaguely he heard the girl scream again, and then after a blinding flash of light somewhere in his brain and a surge of sickening pain, darkness closed in and shut out everything.

Medley came to slowly, aware of an intense throbbing in his head, of a stickiness above his ear that extended down his neck, and of a dull aching in his arm. Unmoving, he listened, allowing his half-open eyes to drift about and take in as much of the camp as possible without revealing his consciousness.

He was alone. That became apparent after several minutes, and gathering his strength, he sat up. He was somewhat dizzy, and for a time he remained in a sitting position while his senses wheeled and spun crazily. When that sensation had ceased, he reached up and tenderly explored the side of his head with his fingertips.

He had been lucky. The outlaw's bullet had just grazed him. It had enough force to knock him senseless and draw a large amount of blood—which was most fortunate, for Sid and the outlaw who had shot him the second time, Payton, had assumed him dead.

He turned his attention to his arm, now stiffening as the anesthetic of shock wore off. It was not a serious wound; Tom had taken a few bullets during his life, and neither of these injuries disturbed him much—far less than the fact that Lucilla Kinkaid was gone, taken by Hazelwood and Payton.

Red Mescole was dead, he was assuming that; he picked up his pistol, caught beneath him when he fell. Reloading the weapon and thrusting it into its holster, he got unsteadily to his feet.

Pausing long enough to let the light-headedness clear, Tom crossed to where his horse was still thethered to a stout piñon tree. Removing the neckerchief he wore, he wet it from the canteen and dabbed at his wounds. Both stung sharply as he endeavored to clean them, and the place in his arm began to bleed again. Wrapping the square of cloth about it, he glanced around.

Anger was now pushing through him. What the hell was he supposed to do now? Go in search of the girl, get her away from the outlaws, or minding his own business, continue to Abilene? Damn it all to hell, why did he have to get mixed up in the thing, anyway? And why should he keep on?

Hazelwood and Payton would not kill Lucilla, he was certain.

Tom's thoughts halted there. How could he be sure? Whatever else he knew about Lucilla, one thing was clear in his mind. She was genuinely afraid of her stepbrother and his outlaw partner— and he had heard Sid promise the girl a beating.

But he had his obligation to Amos Cord to consider. Would it be right to put aside his vow to recover his old friend's sole pride in life and turn his attention to the problems of Lucilla Kinkaid? He owed much to Amos Cord—everything, when you came right down to it; could he ignore that and later on live with the decision?

Moving back into the center of the camp, he collected the cooking gear, the sack of grub, and his wool blanket. He looked about for Lucilla's and, not finding it, guess the girl had taken hers when she left. Loading up, he climbed stiffly onto the bay. At that moment he caught sight of a dusty bundle of cloth at the edge of the cleft, and urging the gelding on, he had a look.

It was Red Mescole. Hazelwood and Payton had made no effort to bury their dead partner, had simply dragged him after removing any valuables from the body, most likely, off into a shallow draw, and taking his horse, they had ridden on.

That display of callousness brought a grimness to Tom Medley, crystallizing any indecision that he harbored concerning aid for Lucilla Kinkaid. He had no choice but to help her.

Taut, he moved out of the camp area and began a slow circuit of the area fronting the slash in the outcropping. Halfway around he came to where the outlaws had picketed their horses, and leaning down, Tom studied the tracks until he located the hoof prints that indicated the point where the men, accompanied by Lucilla and Red Mescole's mount had ridden out. At once Medley began to follow, having an easy time of it for the first quarter mile, for the soil was sandy and loose and the four sets of tracks were quickly visible.

But after a bit Hazelwood, or Payton, led the party up onto the trail that paralleled the mountain, the same one he and Lucilla had followed the night before. The outlaws were making no effort to conceal their tracks, convinced that he was dead, or soon would be, and therefore no threat of any kind; thus Tom Medley was able to move fairly fast.

Nevertheless it was almost midday before he caught sight of them, halted in the meager shadow of a mesquite tree a few yards off the trail. He could see the two men and, beyond them, the horses. A tightness caught at Medley's throat. Where was Lucilla? Had they—?

Tom swore in relief when he saw the girl a short distance farther on. She appeared to be sitting, back to a rock, and it looked as if her hands and feet were tied. Hazelwood and Payton had evidently halted to rest the horses, and not to eat, as there was no fire going.

For several minutes Tom studied the situation, debating with himself the best course to follow. He could move directly in on the outlaws, gun them down from behind, but that didn't appeal to him. He'd already killed one man in a matter that actually didn't concern him. Adding two more by shooting them in the back was out of the question.

He noted then the band of brush bordering an arroyo a short distance to the right of the girl and the outlaws. By circling and riding down into the wash, then following it to where he'd be opposite Lucilla, there was a good chance he could get to her without being seen. Anyway, short of a shootout, it was his best bet.

Favoring his stiff arm, ignoring the throbbing in his head, Medley dropped back from behind the clump of rabbit brush where he had halted, and making a wide circle, he gained the arroyo. Riding down into it, he continued along its twisting, sandy floor to where he figured he'd be abreast the outlaws and Lucilla.

He realized he was nearer than he'd hoped when he caught the sound of one of the horses stamping impatiently. A hard, set grin on his whiskery face, all discomfort from his wounds forgotten, Medley dismounted and, securing the bay gelding to an Apache plume, worked his way through the ragged, prickly growth of weeds to where he could see the outlaws and the girl.

He had come out midway between Lucilla and the two men. He backed up slowly, dropped again into the wash, retreated a half a dozen yards, and once more crawled through the knee-high growth to where he could see the girl.

She was only a wagon-length from him, and as he hesitated behind a globular snakeweed, some sound he made, or perhaps pure intuition, caused Lucilla to look around. Her eyes spread wide in surprise and relief, and then she flung a warning glance at Sid Hazelwood and Payton. Medley shook his head as an indication for her not to worry, and reaching down, he drew his knife from its belt sheath. Holding the blade between his teeth, he resumed the task of silently making his way through the weeds and tufts of squirrel-tail grass.

Drawing close to the girl, Tom quickly slashed the rawhide strips that bound her wrists and ankles, and then motioning for her to stretch out flat, started her toward the arroyo. Waiting until she had slipped over its edge and was beyond view, he turned then to the horses. Her buckskin mare was at the opposite end of the picketed group, which required that Medley drop back a short distance and from there worm a course to the animals.

By then he was sweating furiously. Weeds dug into his body; his head throbbed and his wounded arm ached with redoubled intensity, but he finally reached the point where he could seize the buckskin's reins and pull them free of the bush to which they were attached.

Medley froze, lay motionless. John Payton had got to his feet. Turned from Tom, the ōutlaw pulled off his hat and stretched. Then taking the bottle of whiskey Sid Hazelwood proffered, he put the container to his lips and had a deep swallow of the liquor.

"She'll talk." Hazelwood's voice came clearly to Medley, firm and convinced. "By the time we get back to Arizona—maybe before—she'll be real anxious to talk up."

Tom considered the outlaw's words and wondered at their meaning. They were speaking of Lucilla, of course, but what did they mean about forcing her to talk? His understanding of the matter was that they were afraid she would talk! He swore under his breath. There was more to the story than Lucilla had told him—something she had held back.

Infuriated at being continually kept in the dark by the girl, Medley continued to lie perfectly still in the weeds, ready to use his gun if either of the men looked in his direction and spotted him, or noticed that Lucilla was no longer sitting bound against the embankment. Payton still stood and after a moment helped himself to another pull from the bottle of liquor; then, brushing at his mouth with the back of his hand, he sat down.

Tom waited out a full minute, and then, as the men began a low voiced conversation, he moved off slowly and carefully, still low to the ground, leading the buckskin toward the arroyo. The bank of the wash was too steep where he had made his exit, and it was necessary to continue another ten yards or so before the mare could make a descent to the floor of the wash.

He found Lucilla, the bay in tow, awaiting him. She had seen the problem that he faced with the mare, and recognizing the need for losing no time, she had freed the gelding and, keeping pace with Tom and the buckskin, led the bay down the wash. There was concern on the girl's face as Medley handed the mare's reins to her.

"They shot you. How bad are you hurt? I thought—"

His only response was a brusque shake of the head as he took charge of the bay. Tight-lipped, he motioned for her to mount and, swinging onto the gelding, struck out up the deep arroyo at a fast walk.

9

With luck, Medley figured, they would have several minutes' start before the outlaws discovered the girl's absence—but they should move faster. Nevertheless he kept the horses to a walk until they were a good hundred yards from Sid Hazelwood and Payton, and there at a break in the arroyo wall, he pulled up onto firmer ground and, putting the bay and the buckskin into a fast lope, struck off across the fairly level flat.

They had covered less than a mile when Tom, glancing back, caught sight of the outlaws in pursuit. He drew Lucilla's attention and by pointing made her aware of the oncoming men. She acknowledged with a taut nod. There was no exchange of words, even had he been of a mind; the pound of the horses' hooves on the sun-baked ground made such impossible.

They were heading due north, a course that was taking them farther away from the road to Abilene.

It angered Medley. He was realizing that not only had he now lost the ground made up on Donner and Trigg, but this change he was being forced to make would put him even more behind. And for what? For a girl who had not been honest with him—judging from what he had overheard Payton and Hazelwood say.

Medley swore raggedly under his breath and threw another look at the two riders on their trail. Not only was he in the dark where Lucilla Kinkaid was concerned, but he had killed a man for her sake—and stood a damn good chance of having to kill again, or maybe get killed himself! If she . . .

"They're—they're getting closer!"

Tom heard Lucilla's desperate cry above the sound of the horses, and twisting about in the saddle of the galloping bay, he studied Hazelwood and Payton. They did appear to be nearer. Coming back around, he glanced ahead. They were pulling away from the upper end of the mountain and approaching a dark band of trees—a fairly extensive growth it appeared. He gestured at the grove.

"If we can make it to there, we'll stand a good chance of getting them off our heels," he shouted, and bending lower over the gelding, used his spurs.

The bay responded and began to draw away from the buckskin Lucilla was riding. But the girl was not long in correcting the lapse. Crouching, using the trailing ends of the reins as a whip, she

called on the mare for more speed and shortly
caught up and kept pace with the bay.

Shoulder to shoulder, they reached the first stand
of brush and soon were driving hard into the
shadowy depths of the grove. The horses began to
slow, their progress hindered by the trees and
dense undergrowth.

"Which way?"

Lucilla's voice was strained, her features anxious
as they wove in and out between the cottonwoods
and scrub oaks. Shafts of sunlight were filtering
down through the branches of the trees, lending a
reverent atmosphere to the hushed area.

The horses were now down to a walk. Medley,
glancing about, gave the problem Lucilla had voiced
thought. It would be dangerous to delay for any
length of time, as the outlaws would soon be entering the trees.

Hazelwood and Payton knew they were headed
for Abilene; they had gotten that information from
Donovan in Bear Springs, he realized. Why not
just get out of their way and let them act on their
knowledge? If the outlaws searched through the
grove and failed to find the girl and him, they
undoubtedly would turn east, skirt the upper end
of the mountain, and continue on for the Texas
town—hoping most likely to set an ambush and
intercept Lucilla and him somewhere along the
way.

"Left—west," he said, and turned the bay into
that direction.

Lucilla drew up beside him. "West? That will put you farther behind those horse thieves than ever!"

Tom shrugged, made no reply. He was full aware of what the move would cost him in time and distance, and he had a fleeting wonder if fate, intervening constantly as it was, intended to prevent his recovering the copper-dun stud for Amos Cord.

But that was damn foolishness, he told himself. He'd find the stud, maybe not in Abilene, but somewhere, despite the fact that he had a troublesome girl and two outlaws on his hands; and while that certainly wasn't to his liking, that matter came first.

Keeping the horses at a steady walk, they came finally to the west edge of the grove, and there Tom drew to a halt. Dismounting, he stood motionless, listening, while Lucilla came down off the buckskin. He could hear nothing but the soft moaning of a dove somewhere back in the trees and the barking of prairie dogs in a village off on the flat ahead.

"Do you think they've—" Lucilla began, and broke off abruptly. "Those places where you were shot—hadn't we better do something about them?"

"Later," Medley replied gruffly. "And if you're asking if Sid and his friend have gone on, my guess is that they have."

There were a few questions he wanted to ask the girl, and he intended to get straight answers, but that, too, would have to wait until he was certain he'd gotten the outlaws off their trail.

"They won't give up," she said disconsolately.

"Not expecting them to. I figure when they can't find us, they'll go on for Abilene."

Lucilla nodded. There was a discoloration on her left cheek that he hadn't noticed earlier. Tom's eyes narrowed slightly.

"Sid and Payton rough you up some?"

"Was Sid," Lucilla answered. "He hit me, trying to make me—make me do what he wanted." Raising a hand, she tenderly felt the bruised area with her fingertips. "I've caused you a lot of trouble."

"For damn sure," Medley agreed bluntly, and turned to his horse. "Time we moved on," he added, going into the saddle. "We'll head north a ways, then angle toward the east."

Lucilla, settling herself on the buckskin, said, "Won't that take us even farther off the road to Abilene?"

"Considerable. But there's a shortcut we can take—through Apache country."

She was quiet for a brief time, as if giving the idea deep thought. Then she said in a tentative voice, "It'll be risky going through Indian country—"

"Chance we'll have to take, but we could get lucky and not run into any trouble. Tribes around here are mostly peaceful, except for a party of renegades now and then."

"When will we reach the shortcut?"

Medley glanced over the surrounding country,

taking note of the mountains now to the rear of them, the expanse of black lava plains to the right—the high, dark-blue hills on to the east.

"Tomorrow, I reckon—probably in the afternoon. We'll make camp tonight at the edge of what some folks call the Arenas Blancas, if we can make it that far and don't run into Sid and his partner again."

"Arenas Blancas" Lucilla repeated. "What's that?"

"Words mean white sand. Big stretch of it we'll have to cross to get to the shortcut."

"Sounds like it might be hard going—if it's nothing but sand."

"No worse than the Jornada—the country we just came over."

"Jornada?"

"The Jornada del Muerto—Journey of Death. It's a trail that runs south out of a town called Socorro toward Mexico for eighty or ninety miles. No water or settlements anywhere. Folks going and coming from Mexico used to follow it, but nowadays they usually stick to the road along the river."

"Were we on it? I don't remember—"

"We crossed it, that's all—saw about ten miles of what it's like. . . . Been aiming to ask—"

Tom's words halted abruptly. On to the south two riders had broken into view. He muttered a warning and wheeled immediately in behind a clump of brush. Lucilla, reacting quickly, crowded the mare in close to the bay.

"Could be Hazelwood and Payton," Medley said, pointing. "Right about where they'd be if they struck out due east after losing us in that grove."

The girl leaned forward, studied the distant figures. "Too far to tell for sure, but you're probably right. Do you think they saw us?"

"Doubt it. They'd be coming this way by now if they had. . . . Started to ask you a bit ago about something that's a real puzzlement to me." The anger that had pressed him earlier had faded somewhat and his tone now was kinder and more patient.

Lucilla continued to watch the riders, now disappearing into the low hills and buttes well in the distance.

"You said your stepbrother and his partners were out to kill you so's you couldn't do any talking about them. I can't figure why they didn't this morning when they had a good chance. Instead they just rode off with you."

Lucilla turned to him and then looked down. "I know it all seems strange to you, even suspicious, but there's a reason for it—one I'm not sure you'd understand."

"Try me," Medley suggested flatly.

The outlaws, if that was who the riders were, no longer were in sight, and touching the bay with his spurs, Tom started the bay to moving. Lucilla's buckskin followed at once without any prompting from her.

"I will—just as soon as I get it all straight in my

mind and can explain it so that it makes sense.
Maybe tomorrow or the next day."

Medley frowned, and then his shoulders lifted
and fell indifferently. "Up to you," he said stiffly.

Lucilla brushed at her face with a red bandana
she took from a pocket. "It's so hard to think—
what with Sid and the others sneaking up on us,
the shooting, them taking me away with them,
leaving you laying there dead: I'd all but given up
hope when I saw you coming out of that arroyo.
You cut me loose, and then there were those terri-
ble moments while you led my horse away—only
moments, but they seemed like hours, all during
which I couldn't breathe!

"After that we had to get clear of them, make a
run for it, only to have them chasing us again—
and all the time you'd been shot, and your wounds
hadn't been taken care of, still haven't because we
can't stop long enough to do anything about them.
There's hardly been a minute's peace for us, and
now with them down there—ahead—"

"We'll stay clear of them," he said, reassuring
her.

"Oh, I hope so! What about those wounds?"

"Not bothering me much. Arm's a mite stiff and
I've had a spell or two of light-headedness."

"Can we stop soon so's I can look at them, see
what I can do?"

Medley pointed to a dark-green blur in the far
distance. "That's a grove. There's a creek running

87

through it, near as I recollect. Ought to get there around dark. Can make camp then."

"Good. I don't have any kind of medicine, but I can clean the wounds and find something for bandages. We've got to keep the places from mortifying until we can get to a doctor."

"Could be a far piece," Tom replied.

He hadn't given the wounds much thought, time and mind being occupied by more pressing matters, but he reckoned something should be done about them. As far as medicine and the attention of a doctor were concerned, they were out of the question; they were days from any settlement where such was available.

Medley remembered then the bottle of whiskey he had purchased along with other trail supplies at Solomon's General Store. He'd turn it over to Lucilla when she went to work on him. Liquor, he knew from experience, was a good disinfectant.

10

They saw no more of Hazelwood and Payton, and shortly after the sun had sunk into a flare of gold in the west, they pulled to a halt beside a shallow, narrow creek that, as Tom had remembered, wound its way through the trees.

The vast area of white sand over which they must cross was still a distance to the east—a fact that pleased Tom Medley. It was better to start across the Arenas Blancas in the early-morning hours when the heat and the blinding glare were not so pitiless.

In the small clearing where they had stopped Tom unloaded supplies, and then picketing the horses close to the stream, he returned to build a fire for Lucilla, and attend to other camp-making chores. The girl elected first to see to his wounds, heating up a can of water to the boiling point, and then with strips and pads of white cotton cloth procured from some garment she was wearing, she carefully cleaned the crusted places.

"I just wish I had something to disinfect with and some salve to help the wounds heal," she murmured when she was finished.

Tom pointed at his saddlebags. "I've got a bottle of whiskey—"

Lucilla arose at once, obtained the liquor, and returning to him, poured a quantity on each of the two pads she had formed. Tom's arm had been aching while steadily stiffening throughout the way, and the narrow groove on the side of his head where Payton's bullet had laid a stinging furrow still smarted; but neither produced the sheer pain that the application of raw whiskey did when Lucilla put the soaked pads in place and bound them firmly with bandages.

He swore grimly, smiled. "Getting shot feels better."

The woman ignored his wry comment. "Expect the liquor will keep the wounds from mortifying, but we best go see a doctor first chance we get."

"Can't much figure on that till we get to Abilene," he said, drawing on his shirt.

Turning away, Medley began to collect more wood for the fire. They need take no particular care as far as the smoke and glare were concerned, he figured; they were still miles from Apache country, and when they had last seen Sid

Hazelwood and his partner, the pair was well to the south.

Lucilla, taking her time, prepared a satisfying if not varied supper, and not long after the meal was over, they both rolled up in their blankets and were quickly asleep. Tom had wanted to continue questioning the girl, get the truth from her where the outlaws were concerned, but she appeared much too tired to talk and he was but little better off. It could wait until tomorrow, Medley decided.

They awoke to the slight chill of early morning, rose, and each went wordlessly about the routine of chores they had slipped into—Tom building a fire and then getting the horses prepared for the day's traveling, Lucilla cooking the meal and seeing to the bedrolls.

They had just begun to eat when movement at the edge of the clearing caught Medley's eye. Scarcely moving his head, he looked toward the movement. The muscles of his jaw tightened. Five Apache braves were standing along the fringe of brush encircling the camp. Beyond them were their horses.

"Indians," he murmured quietly. "Don't look up. Let on like you don't know they're there."

Lucilla stiffened at his cautioning words, but she continued to stir the concoction of salt pork, beans, onions, and potatoes in the spider as though nothing was wrong.

Moving slowly, Tom got to his feet. He turned

to face the braves. They were far off their usual range, which was not reassuring. These would be renegades, likely, outcasts from the tribe they belonged to. Crossing his arms so that the weapon on his hip was not only more visible to them, but quickly available should he have to use it, he nodded.

All were young men dressed only in breechcloth and leggings, and all but one wore a ragged white band about their heads to keep their hair in place; the fifth had chosen a faded red bandanna for that purpose. Their skins shone dull copper in the half-light working its way down through the branches of the trees, and their small black eyes were like bits of jet. Each had a rifle. He'd have no chance against the five of them should trouble start, Tom realized; the best answer was to treat them as friends.

"Brothers," he called. "You are welcome to our camp."

The Apaches exchanged glances. One, a short, stocky brave, shook his head. *"No comprendo."*

Tom shrugged. He should have remembered that Apaches spoke Spanish along with their native tongue. But that didn't help much; he knew very little Spanish.

"Aquí—comer," he said, reaching for the spider and offering it to them.

The brave with the red bandanna and the husky one beside him moved forward. Each dipped a hand into the mixture in the frying pan, juggled the hot semiliquid about briefly, and then stuffed it into their mouths. A guttural word exploded from both, and grimacing, they spat the mixture into the fire.

Lucilla had risen to her feet. Her features were drawn and Medley knew she was frightened, but the girl was not permitting it to show. The Indian wearing the bandanna looked at her with interest and, reaching out, fingered a strand of her hair straying from beneath her hat. Instantly Tom stepped in close and knocked the Apache's hand away.

"*Mi esposa,*" he said, making a display of anger.

The brave's dark eyes flared and he dropped into a threatening half-crouch. At that moment one of the three still standing at the edge of the clearing barked something in their own language and the Apache sullenly turned away.

The squat member of the party made a motion as if drinking. "Whiskey—you got?"

Tom shook his head. "No whiskey. Coffee."

The Indian spat again, said something to his friends. Then, "You hunt?"

"No," Medley replied, once more shaking his head. "Ride far—to Abilene."

He didn't know if the braves had ever heard of the settlement or not, but it was clear what they were driving at. So many settlers had come into the Indian's country hunting deer and the lesser animals that food for the tribes had become a problem.

"Abilene," the squat brave repeated, pronouncing each syllable distinctly.

"Yes—Abilene. White-man town. We go."

The Apaches greeted his words with silence, simply stared, leaving in Medley's mind the question of whether he had been successful in explaining his and Lucilla's presence in the grove. But he said no more, only waited, conscious of the building tension.

Abruptly the heavy-set Indian spoke to his friends. All wheeled and started for their horses—all, that is, but the one who had taken a liking for Lucilla. He hesitated, his sharp gaze first on the girl, then on Tom, and back to Lucilla. Medley allowed his hand to slide down and rest on the butt of his pistol. It was an offhand, indifferent gesture, but the brave clearly understood its meaning; the white man would fight and kill for his woman, if necessary.

"They're leaving," Lucilla whispered in a strained voice—one both of surprise and relief.

"Maybe. You can't ever bet on Indians. That one who took a fancy to you—I'm not sure about him," Tom replied, watching the braves vault onto their ponies.

"What had we better do?"

"Take it slow and easy," Medley said. Lucilla was trembling, reaction now setting in. "Make it look like you're going to go right ahead and eat—"

"I—I can't swallow a bite—I'm so frightened—"

"Then start getting the pans and stuff together. Don't hurry. Biggest mistake we could make right now is let them think we're scared."

"Do you want to eat?"

"Kind of lost my appetite, too—leastwise for the time being."

The braves were cutting their ponies about and pulling away. Tom dropped to a crouch beside the girl and began to assist her in getting things ready for leaving by dumping the coffee and the stewlike mixture in the frying pan into the fire and stacking the pans.

"I'll bring up the horses," he said when that was done, and rising, moved off to where their mounts were waiting.

He had lost sight of the Apaches when they rode off into the grove, and he had no way of knowing if the entire party had departed, or if the one who had left reluctantly was still hanging about. He'd have to take a chance on that possibility, but if the brave was close by and made an effort at claiming Lucilla as his prize, he'd be ready for him.

Reaching the horses, Tom led them back to the edge of the clearing. Lucilla had everything stored in the saddlebags and flour sack, ready to go. Tense, Medley loaded them onto the horses and motioned for Lucilla to mount up.

"Get in front of me," he said, swinging onto the bay. Pointing into the direction opposite of that taken by the Indians, he added, "Head that way—and make as little noise as you can. I don't know for sure where the hell they are."

11

Medley and Lucilla moved hurriedly but carefully through the trees and brush. Tom continually watched for signs of the Apaches, not at all convinced that he and the girl were going to get off so easily. What particularly worried him was the interest the brave wearing the red bandanna about his head had taken in Lucilla. If trouble came, he likely would be the one who incited it.

"How long will it take to get where we won't have to worry about Indians?" the girl asked a time later. Now riding at Medley's side, she had been silent from the moment they had left the camp and only spoke now in a low voice.

Tom knew his reply would be of no comfort to her, but he could see no sense in denying her the truth. It was better that she know exactly their situation.

"Be a couple of days for sure. Apaches roam

pretty much all through here. Comanches, too—now and then."

She sighed heavily. "I thought they were peaceable and weren't bothering folks anymore."

Tom looked ahead. A lightness was appearing through the maze of brush and trees: the Arenas Blancas—a world of glittering white sand. He had hoped to reach and cross it earlier when the reflected sunlight was not so intense, but his timing had been off.

"Most are," he replied, answering the girl's question. "Problem is the tribes have renegades and outlaws among them, same as the white people."

Abruptly Medley raised a hand for silence and halted. Lucilla also drew up sharply, both alarm and question in her eyes.

"Something—or somebody—over there to the right," Tom said in a whisper.

Lucilla turned her attention to the indicated direction. "Is it the Apaches—the ones we saw back there early this morning?" she asked, her voice equally low.

He shook his head, eyes still fastened to the brush where he had spotted movement. "Hard telling, but it could be. Might have changed their minds about letting us be, and started hunting us."

Lucilla glanced about as if searching for a place to hide. "Hadn't we better try to find—"

"Just set tight. Maybe they'll head the other way. Can you shoot a pistol?"

"Some. I'm not very good with one, but I know how to use it."

Moving cautiously, Medley half-turned, unbuckled the saddlebag on the bay's right flank, and dug out the spare weapon he carried. It was old, had been replaced by the newer model pistol he now carried, but it was in good, reliable condition. Muffling the sound, he flipped open the loading gate and quietly thumbed cartridges into five of the cylinder chambers, set the hammer on the one left empty, and passed the heavy forty-five to the woman.

"Be a good idea for you to carry this," he said.

Lucilla grasped the weapon firmly and thrust it under the waistband of the trousers she was wearing. "Could I have some extra cartridges?"

Tom grinned despite the precarious moments and, producing a dozen additional brass-jacketed shells, passed them to her. Lucilla Kinkaid was a woman any man could be proud to have at his side.

Suddenly two Indians appeared in front of the shadowy brush where he had seen movement. One was the brave who wore the red bandanna about his head, the other was the short, stocky man. They had evidently split from the rest of the party and gone off on their own—no doubt to search for him and the girl, Tom reckoned. From the corner of an eye he saw Lucilla's hand drop to the pistol she now carried.

"Easy," he murmured. "Don't want to do any shoothing unless we have to. But if it comes down to it, we can handle this pair."

It was a statement timed to reassure Lucilla, but he also meant it. The danger lay in what would come after the gunplay if it became necessary to shoot it out with the two braves. Gunshots would surely bring the rest of the renegades, possibly others that were in the area, and for Lucilla and him to try and make a stand against several Apaches attacking in their efficient, near invisible way would be hopeless.

The braves remained motionless, evidently undecided as to which direction they should take. And then they moved out, cutting left through the trees and undergrowth.

"They're coming this way," Lucilla murmured, her voice taut.

Medley reached out and laid a hand on her arm. It was the wounded member and the side effort sent a twinge of pain through him, but he ignored it.

"They'll cross in front of us," he said, hoping to allay her fears. "It'll be maybe fifty or sixty feet away. If our horses don't act up, they'll never know we are here."

"But if they do—if they start toward us—shall I shoot?"

Tom nodded. "Won't have no choice. You take

the one that'll be to your left—and point your gun at the biggest part of him, his belly. I'll handle the other one. When the shootings over, get out of here fast—ride like hell because the shots'll bring the rest of them."

Lucilla signified her understanding, and then in the deep, tense hush she added, "Which way? We may get separated."

"We won't—I'll see to that. But we're heading east. Just head straight for the sun. . . . Careful—"

The two braves had broken into an opening among the trees fifty yards or so in front of them. Both were leaning forward on their mounts studying the ground as if searching for a trail or some signs of passage of the horses of those they were seeking. The silence that filled the grove seemed to deepen, become more oppressive as tension mounted.

And then abruptly the Apaches were gone. They had entered the dense growth bordering the clearing into which they had ridden. Medley raised himself cautiously in his stirrups as he endeavored to follow their course.

"Going north," he said after a bit. "We'll give them about five minutes and move on. Don't want to hold off too long, though—it just might come to them that they're on the wrong track and start them doubling back."

They waited out the specified length of time, and then, after making certain the braves had not reversed their course and were nowhere in view,

Lucilla and Tom continued on their way, reaching, a short time later, the vast expanse of white sand.

"Do we have to cross this?" Lucilla wondered, awed by the sight. "Can't we go around it?"

"Be a long ride either direction—and we haven't got the time. I figure we're about at the narrowest part, which puts us six or eight miles from here to the other side. Can cover that pretty fast."

"But what about those Apaches? Won't they see us once we're out there in the open? There's no bushes, no trees, no cover of any kind, just a kind of rolling prairie—"

"Chance we'll have to take. Wind's blowing out there a bit, so pull your neckerchief up over your mouth and nose to keep out the dust and sand. And best you tip your hat over your eyes—it'll help some in cutting down the glare."

Medley, following his own advice, waited while the girl made the suggested adjustments, and then led off. For the first quarter mile or so the horses managed with little difficulty, but after they had gotten well out into the dunes, drifts, and undulating flats, their pace slowed as their hooves sank and dragged in the glistening, loose gypsum particles.

Midway Tom heard a cry of alarm from Lucilla, riding on his left. "It's the Apaches! They've seen us!"

Medley swung his attention to the left. A quarter mile or so away the two braves were just surging out of the underbrush and breaking out onto the first stretch of sand. Tom glanced over his shoulder.

"Too late to turn back," he said. "Only thing we can do is run for it. Their horses can't do any better in this loose sand than ours."

At once Medley raked the bay with spurs and sent him lunging ahead. Lucilla dropped back briefly, and then urging the little buckskin mare on by drumming her heels into the horse's flanks, soon regained her place alongside Medley.

"Looks like they're gaining on us—"

Tom nodded grimly at the girl's cry. "Could be. There are solid places in the sand where the footing's better for the horses. They must be on one of them," he said, and then added, "Leave it to a damn Apache to know where those strips are."

Almost at once their own mounts broke out onto a firmer area and their speed increased noticeably. Medley cast a look at the braves. They appeared now to have encountered just the opposite, for their horses had slowed and were laboring in the slack surface.

"Not much farther," Tom called to the girl a short time later.

Patches of brown were showing in the white sand ahead of them, and here and there clumps of weeds and low brush were to be seen.

"We're going to beat them," Lucilla cried, her voice now light and hopeful.

They would—and by considerable distance,

thanks to the effect of bad footing for the Apache ponies. But gaining the solid ground and the undergrowth on the east side of the Arenas Blancas would not mean the race was over. Despite their worn horses, they must continue on making as good a time as possible, leaving as few signs of their passage as they could. The Apaches would not give up.

"Can you keep going?" he asked minutes later when, with the sand behind them, they were moving along at a good pace through the low, weedy growth of a flat.

"I can—" Lucilla's reply was barely audible as she glanced back over her shoulder.

The renegades were not in sight and there was no way of determining if they were still out on the dazzling sand or had gained the solid footing of the prairie.

"Best we ride as far as we can—try to get them off our trail before we stop," Tom explained.

"I can make it," the girl answered, a stubborn lift in her voice.

Tom, tension in him fading, grinned. Lucilla would, too—but he wasn't so sure about the buckskin. The hard going through the miles of loose gypsum had taken a lot out of the mare, and Medley knew his own horse would need to rest soon. But both mounts would have to continue for a while.

Their pace became slower, and somewhere around midafternoon it had dropped to a walk.

Still Medley did not call a halt. There were no signs of the Apache braves—still somewhere behind them, he was certain—but he and Lucilla were now on the Apache Reservation, and there was better than a good chance they would encounter more braves, some of whom could prove to be friendly and some who would not.

The latter kind were more likely. Though they might not be renegades, as the others apparently were, they quite rightfully resented any and all white men being on their assigned area. They had been pushed around for so many years that it was only natural for them to make a stand and resist what they considered trespass on their property.

Late in the day the horses reached their limit. To ride them any farther would be dangerous. Acutely aware of this, Medley began to look for a place to halt and camp until midnight or so.

Finally an arroyo appeared, and turning into it, he followed the somewhat shallow gash in the prairie for a short distance and pulled to a stop in a fairly wide, brushy cutback. There was a wealth of plume and rabbitbrush that not only screened the ravine from a casual passerby, but also, green thick on the slope above, offered a place where Tom Medley could set up a watch over the surrounding country for the Apaches.

"I'll see to the horses," he said as he came wearily off the saddle. "Don't bother to fix any supper until you've rested a bit."

Fatigue dragging at her features and showing in

her every movement, Lucilla got off the buckskin and took the flour sack of supplies from him as well as the saddlebag containing the cooking and eating utensils and laid them on a nearby rock.

"I expect you're hungry—"

Tom nodded. "Been a long time since supper last night," he said, "but I can hold out for a bit. We'll be here awhile—till midnight anyway."

Lucilla began to delve into the sack of trail grub. "We'd best not build a fire, I guess."

"No—could be spotted by those two braves. Besides, we're on the Apache Reservation. Sure don't want to do anything that'd draw attention."

12

They slept for a time, Lucilla rolled up in her blanket alongside the wall of the ravine that flowed into the arroyo, Tom Medley above on the slope where he could maintain a fitful watch for Apaches who might be prowling the area.

Not long after midnight he descended to the floor of the wash and, going for the horses, readied them for the long day that lay ahead. They appeared rested, both benefiting from the last of the grain Tom had bought earlier and now divided equally between them. He watered them sparingly from the supply in the canteens as there would be no more available until they reached a spring—hopefully still flowing—at the end of the day.

Such chores finished, Medley roused the girl, and mounting up, they rode off into the moonlit night. It was pleasant. They followed no specific trail, but let the horses pick their way on a southeasterly course through the brush and scrub trees, along the arroyos and washes, and over the short, rolling hills.

"Are we still in Apache country?" Lucilla asked an hour or so later as they pressed on.

Tom glanced about, shrugged. "Probably—kind of hard to tell. But even if we are, there's no guarantee we won't run into another bunch. Reservation boundaries don't mean much to them."

Lucilla stirred in the saddle, drew her jacket closer about her slender body to ward off the night's chill. "I'll be so thankful when we get to Abilene and can stop worrying about Indians," she said. "How far are we from there?"

"Be a guess, but I'd say about a week—"

"A week!" the young woman echoed. "I thought we were a lot nearer than that."

"Had to swing a few miles out of our way," Tom explained. "Cost us some time."

He could have added that such would not have been necessary if they hadn't encountered Sid Hazelwood and his partners, but Medley made no mention of it. Lucilla would know why they had lost time.

And they could lose more. Tom again checked their back trail for any sign of the Apache braves—or others who might have heard them as they crossed the reservation, and come to investigate. Although the night was bright and visibility was good, the brush and trees restricted his view to little more than a dozen or so yards in each direction.

Tom could neither hear nor see any riders, but he took no assurance from that and gave thought as to how he would face any unexpected attack. Should a party of braves burst suddenly out of the shadows, he could do but one thing: use his forty-five. If it proved to be a large party, he probably couldn't hold them off for long, even with Lucilla firing the weapon he had given her, but he'd do the best he could.

Lucilla . . . He let his mind settle on her as the horses plodded woodenly on. He was still not certain of what was going on where Hazelwood and his partners—now only one—were concerned. Several things she had told him appeared to be untrue, but there was no doubt she was in serious trouble of some kind; otherwise the outlaws would not have kidnapped her and kept her tied hand and foot.

Why was Lucilla reluctant to tell him about it? A man would think that she, after being befriended and protected by him, would take him into her confidence. As well get to the bottom of it right here and now, Medley decided suddenly, and put his attention on the girl.

She was slumped in her saddle, chin sunk into her chest, body moving gently to and fro with the motion of the buckskin mare—sleeping soundly. Tom studied her briefly and turned away. That Lucilla was near exhaustion from tension, the hard riding, and lack of rest he was well aware. He'd not awaken her, but let her sleep. There would be plenty of time before reaching Abilene to find out what it was all about.

A rattling in the brush on beyond Lucilla brought Tom Medley to instantaneous alert. Hand resting on the butt of his pistol, he held his eyes to the spot where the noise had seemingly come from. Indians? He gave that a few moment's thought and dismissed the possibility. No Apache brave would be so careless while sneaking up on an enemy as to create such a disturbance. The outlaws—Hazelwood and Payton? Tom had no idea where they might be other than somewhere on to the south of Lucilla and him—but of course, he could be wrong about that. They could have doubled back. . . .

Abruptly a horse walked into view. Riderless, a ragged saddle hanging half off its back, the bridle dangling loosely, leather bleached and broken with only short stubs of the reins still attached to the bit, the animal was little more than skin and bones.

Tom, riding forward, reached out and grasped the headstall of Lucilla's mare, brought her to a halt. As the girl, startled, came awake, Medley slipped from the saddle and walked slowly to the stray.

"What is it?" Lucilla asked anxiously, and then when she caught sight of the abandoned horse, added, "Where do you suppose it came from?"

Tom, approaching the animal carefully, now standing dully in the belly-high undergrowth, did not reply. The stray would likely spook easily, and

110

he wanted to get a firm grip on what was left of the bridle before the animal could bolt.

He reached the horse, a black, and now moving fast, he seized one of the strips of reins. The stray's head snapped up, and alarmed, he made a brief effort at backing away, and halted.

"Hard to answer that," Medley said then to the girl's question. "Expect he belonged to some pilgrim riding through here that run into trouble."

"Probably Apaches or outlaws," Lucilla suggested, watching as Tom drew his skinning knife.

"That'd be a safe bet," he admitted. "Looks like blood on the saddle, all old and dried up." Using his blade, he cut the rope cinch and let the battered hull drop to the ground.

"What are you going to do with him?" the girl wondered as Medley, aware in that moment that his arm was no longer encumbered by stiffness, and that he had long since stopped noticing the pain in his head, worked over the stray. "We don't want him, do we?"

Tom said, "No," and cut the headstall. Immediately the bit came out of the black's mouth and the bridle fell into the brush at his feet.

"At least he can graze and drink now without all that gear on him," Lucilla commented.

Medley retraced his steps to the bay and mounted. "Surprises me some that the Apaches haven't come across him."

"You'd think they would have," Lucilla agreed

as they moved on. Her voice brightened. "Could that mean we're off their reservation?"

The same thought had occurred to Tom. It was hard to believe that a horse could wander around for days, or most likely weeks—judging from the condition of the animal and its gear—without meeting with a brave or a hunting party.

"Sure could be it," he said. "We cut across a bottom corner of their land. Maybe we covered it faster than I figured."

Tom glanced back. The stray had moved forward a few steps and was nuzzling about in the brush for grass. It would be easier now for the horse to survive, barring death from wolves or mountain lions.

Medley resumed his position and looked ahead. The pale lightness above the eastern horizon was growing stronger. Daybreak was not far off.

"We'll pull up at sunrise, fix some breakfast, and rest awhile," he said.

Lucilla twisted about in her saddle, small lines of concern pulling at the smooth, even planes of her face.

"Are you sure it's safe? Maybe we're still in Apache country—"

"Don't think we are, but it's a chance we've got to take," Medley replied. "The horses have to rest. They only had a few hours last night after a hard day. And we both need some grub. Sure can't keep going without a square meal now and then."

Lucilla said no more, and an hour or so later,

when they came to a stop in a shallow coulee, she got busy at once preparing food. There was no spring or creek anywhere nearby, and again they had to draw on the canteens for their needs while allotting a cupful or so to each horse.

"We'll be out by tonight," Lucilla said as she made coffee. "What will we do for—"

"By tonight we'll reach the Pecos River," Tom assured her. "We'll find all the water we need," and then recalling the condition in which they'd found the Rio Grande, out of its banks due to spring rain, added, "Could even be more than we bargain for."

Medley was right. The Pecos was at flood stage, running hard and fast, and out of its usual confines in many places when they reached it late that afternoon.

"How can we cross over?" Lucilla wondered. "I don't know much about it but I doubt if the horses can swim that. The current is too swift."

Tom had to agree. "There's a ford on to the south a few miles. River flattens out for a ways and folks usually do their crossing without any trouble. We might as well keep going till we get there. Be dark by then, so we can make camp and cross over in the morning."

Lucilla said nothing, simply urged the weary buckskin into motion. Medley moved in beside her, and together they pointed their horses downstream on the trail following the course of the surging, silt-laden river, which ran in an almost straight line in that particular section.

"I think I see riders," Lucilla said later, breaking the silence that had claimed her for the better part of an hour. And then, her voice falling in frustration, she continued, "I—I'm not sure, but I think—"

"You'd be right if you're thinking it's Hazelwood and Payton," Medley cut in. "They're at the ford— waiting for us."

13

Halted in the willows along the roily stream, Tom Medley, bitterness at this new delay turning him grim, studied the two outlaws. They were in behind a thick clump of brush a short distance this side of the ford. It was apparent they expected Lucilla and him to come in on the road.

Medley swore feelingly at low breath. It seemed to him, as it had before, that luck conspired against him—that everything possible was happening to keep him from overtaking Rufe Donner and Ike Trigg and recovering Amos Cord's copper-dun stud.

"Do we have to go back?" he heard Lucilla say exhaustedly.

Tom's wide shoulders lifted and fell. He looked leaner, taller, and the growth of beard that now covered the lower half of his face was a dark shadow in the lowering light.

"No, we won't go back—we'll have to cross the

river at the ford. It's the only place I know of other'n the one up in the High Lonesome country—and that's a far piece from here. Going there would cost me—us another week."

Lucilla did not miss the slip in the use of the pronoun. "I'm sorry to be causing you so much trouble—I know you're in a hurry to get to Abilene." She paused, glanced to the west, where the sun was sinking into a flare of gold and red glory. "Maybe it would be best if you'd leave me—go on by yourself."

He could, Tom thought, but he wasn't about to. The thought of leaving Lucilla there on the bank of the flooding Pecos River, days from any town and with the two men she feared so greatly less than a mile away, was the last thing he would ever do. Besides, he'd sort of gotten used to having her around, and it occurred to him now that when they finally did reach Abilene and she went on to Fort Worth, he'd miss her.

Glancing at her—so quiet, so serene, the beauty of her features and the blueness of her eyes enhanced by the soft, fading sunlight—he shook his head.

"Hell with that," he said gruffly, and instantly wished his manner of speaking hadn't been so abrupt.

"I've done nothing but hinder you—"

"Seems we've done some talking along this line before," Medley cut in. "I'd as soon not hear any more of it."

His attention now was on the river and the country adjacent to the ford. Along the surging stream there was a scarcity of brush, only a scattering of weeds, and an occasional small stand of willows—none of which offered concealment for a horse even without a rider. They could forget reaching the ford by following the riverbank.

But they had another choice—risky but possible. Under cover of darkness and despite the bright moonlight, they just might get past Hazelwood and John Payton unnoticed if they were careful. Tom gave it consideration, finally admitted to himself it was their only option.

"We'll stay put here until after dark," he said, coming off the saddle and stretching to relieve his aching muscles. "Then I figure we can drop back, circle wide around Sid and his friend, and come in at the lower end of the ford."

Dismounting, Lucilla glanced at the sky doubtfully. "If it's like it was last night, it won't be dark for long. The moon came out so bright and—"

"Have to chance it. We'll keep low, duck in behind every bit of cover we come to. Horses will be the biggest problem—no way we can hide them. Means we'll have to make a wide circle, stay as far from Sid and Payton as we can."

Lucilla understood, and an hour later they were aboard their horses, and staying close to the dark water of the swiftly flowing Pecos, they headed back upstream.

"I remember there was a ridge about a mile on,"

Medley explained. "We get behind it, can then work our way west easy."

They reached the rise in only a few minutes, swung into its shadow, and pointed west. It was still light, a sort of amber haze covering the land, and Tom knew there was a possibility the outlaws would see them. But the two men had apparently been unaware of the arrival of Lucilla and him earlier—their attention being centered on the main road—so the odds that the outlaws would not see them when they doubled back were all in their favor.

As they rode in behind the rise, Medley had paused to give the two men, crouched before a small fire preparing their evening meal, careful scrutiny. Nothing was very definite at that distance and in the faltering light, but it was easy to see that the outlaws had made their camp on the river beside some brush, thus making themselves more or less invisible to anyone approaching the Pecos from the west. Again they showed no signs of having spotted Lucilla and Tom, and thus reassured, he and the girl had hurried on along the weedy ridge.

They continued west for a good mile and a half, and there began a wide, curving course to the south, crossing the main road a time later, and continuing in the same direction, they eventually cut back to the Pecos a considerable distance below the encamped outlaws.

"I can't see them," Lucilla remarked when they

118

halted on the bank of the river and came off their saddles.

"We're a far piece below them," Medley replied. They were well down the lower end of the ford, too, he saw, in a stretch where the Pecos was narrow, but in its present flood stage it would be too deep to cross.

"We'll have to go back upriver," he said. "We can't ford here. Horses would never make it."

"But won't we run the chance of Sid and Payton seeing us?"

"Maybe," he admitted. "Nothing else we can do—and we'll have to do it tonight."

With a little good luck—which Tom reminded himself he hadn't seen much of—they should be able to cross the Pecos without being spotted by the outlaws. In spite of the strong moonlight, anyone in the water would not be too noticeable. He'd send Lucilla out ahead of him and be ready with his gun to discourage the outlaws if they happened to see her.

They came to a low place a couple of hundred yards below the junction of the road and the river. Even crossing at that established ford would be dangerous, Medley realized. But attempting to gain the opposite bank at any other place would be even riskier. It could be done, however, if the horses could be kept calm and headed into the right direction. That was the source of most trouble and most drownings during a crossing: permitting a horse to turn about and make an effort to return to shore.

"Won't find no better place than here to cross," Tom said, gazing out over the tumbling surface of the river. "Have you ever forded a river on a horse before?"

Lucilla shook her head. Her features were drawn and for the first time Medley thought he recognized fear.

"No big job. Let your horse do the work. When you get out in the middle where it's deep, slip out of the saddle and grab the buckskin's tail and let her tow you. Main thing is—don't let her try to turn back."

"How can I do that?"

"Have to work yourself up to her head if she tries coming around. Grab a rein or the headstall and keep her nose pointed for the other bank. If it's kind of close, she'll get the idea quick and keep going."

Lucilla faced him. "Will you be close to me?"

"Just as close as I can get," Medley said as they went back into the saddle. "Be sure you've got everything on your saddle tied down," he added, checking his own gear. "Fast as that current is, it'll wash anything loose away."

The water would ruin most of their grub anyway, he knew, but there was no help for that. Once on the other side of the river and clear of the outlaws, they could halt, dry out, salvage what was still usable, and replace what was not at the next town.

The mare balked as she waded into the swirling, muddy water but continued on when Medley crowded her hind quarters with the bay, an old hand at crossing rivers. With the girl a stride ahead of him, Tom kept as close a watch as possible upstream. He could not see Hazelwood or Payton, had only a general idea where they had set up their camp, for their fire was no longer visible; but so far there was no activity in the area. It would appear that he and Lucilla were crossing unnoticed.

They reached midstream with the river lashing angrily at the horses. Abruptly the mare stepped off into deeper water. Her head came up and she began to flounder.

"Get off the saddle," Tom called, keeping his voice calm and level in an effort to keep the girl from panicking. "Grab on to your horse's tail."

Too, Medley was careful not to raise his voice any more than necessary lest the outlaws overhear. But he could no longer keep an eye in their direction. Lucilla had come off the struggling mare, was being swept slowly away from the frightened animal. Recovering herself, the girl began to fight her way back, managing after several breathless moments to seize a stirrup.

Tom, off the bay, now having his problems in the racing current, allowed the big gelding to thrash his way up beside the buckskin and took a firm hold on the horses tail as it surged by.

"Hang on," Medley called to the girl as the bay,

stronger and with longer legs than the mare, began to pull ahead. "You're doing fine."

Lucilla, water slapping at her face, made no reply. The mare luckily had made no attempt to change course, and now, with the bay's reassuring presence at her side, continued on for the east bank of the river, only a few yards away.

Suddenly Tom Medley became aware of gunshots flatting hollowly through the night. His mouth pulled down into a tight line. The outlaws had discovered them, were shooting. He had hoped that he and Lucilla would make it to the opposite side of the Pecos without being seen by Hazelwood and Payton and that they could resume the journey to Abilene without fear of being pursued— but luck had gone against them once again.

He could see no signs of the bullets striking the water around them, guessed the outlaws were using pistol and not rifles, which would have had the necessary longer range.

The mare's front hooves hit solid ground first despite the fact the bay was a neck ahead of her. And then, moments later, both horses had gained secure footing and were splashing their way through shallow water to shore. Reaching the bank, Tom and Lucilla released their hold on the horses, and water coursing off them, they climbed up onto solid ground.

"I—I couldn't grab on to my horse's tail—only a stirrup," Lucilla said as if an explanation was in order.

Medley smiled at her unexpected words. "Tail or stirrup—you made it, and that's all I give a damn about!"

Rivulets of water still pouring off them, they stood beside the horses staring at each other in the streaming moonlight, and then Tom shifted his attention to the far side of the river. There had been no more shooting after the first scattered reports, the outlaws evidently realizing that the distance was too great and that it was a waste of ammunition.

"They saw us, didn't they?" Lucilla said. She was shivering, the wet clothing she wore now beginning to chill her.

"Took a few shots," he replied, "but we were too far away. . . . Best we move out. I don't know whether they'll try to ford the river or wait for daylight, but one thing's for damn sure—we got to get you to where you can shuck those wet duds and warm up."

14

They mounted and moved on at once, crossing a barren strip of land that paralleled the river in that area, reaching finally a section where vegetation, while not dense or of any height, did offer cover should Sid Hazelwood and John Payton be following.

Lucilla was chilled to the bone, chattering when she tried to speak and shaking uncontrollably when Medley halted in a small pocket in the brush. Climbing off the bay, he directed the girl to dismount also.

"Be getting out of those wet clothes while I build a fire," he directed.

Hesitating, the girl considered him narrowly. Tom glanced up from where he was raking dry twigs and leaves into a pile. Seeing her concern, he shook his head.

"Don't worry none—you're safe with me," he assured her, and added, "If you can wait a couple of minutes till I get this fire going, I'll take your blanket and stretch it between a couple of bushes. You can get in behind it to shed your clothes."

Lucilla nodded gratefully. Then, "The fire— aren't you afraid Sid and Payton will see the glare and come?"

"Thought of that, but I figure getting you dry is more important," Medley said, and digging into a side pocket of his pants, he procured the oilskin pack in which he carried matches. Striking one against a nearby rock, he put the small flame to the dry tinder and shortly had a fire going.

"That feels so good," Lucilla said, moving in close to the leaping flames.

"Does at that," Tom replied, pausing to extend his hands over the surging warmth. Wet to the skin also, he, too, was feeling the cold, but it bothered him less than it did the girl, he knew. He'd dry off after he'd made Lucilla comfortable.

Turning to the buckskin, Medley removed the girl's blanket roll and, untying the cord with which it was bound, opened it. Despite the tight roll the wool cover was soaked clear through; but he had expected nothing different, and crossing to the edge of the small clearing toward which a faint breeze was carrying the heat and smoke, he hung the blanket across several clumps of oak brush and turned to the bay.

"Throw me your clothes so I can put them close to the fire," he said, removing his own blanket roll and unfurling it. "I'll dry out my blanket much as

I can, and you can wrap it about yourself until your duds are ready to put back on."

Reluctantly Lucilla forsook the fire and stepped in behind the suspended cover. Tom, extending his blanket—fortunately not as soaked as Lucilla's—to its full length, moved in close to the fire and there held the woolen cover as near the flames as prudent.

Bit by piece the girl's sodden clothing began to appear on top of the screen, and when Medley judged she had removed all she deemed necessary, or intended to, he handed his blanket over the screen to her and began to collect her clothing. He heard her murmur with pleasure.

"Your blanket—it's so warm—and it got wet only along one edge. I don't understand—"

"Had my slicker around it," Tom replied, busy draping the girl's garments on surrounding bushes.

Lucilla appeared at that moment. She was wrapped completely in the wool cover, was holding it in place with both hands. Tom nodded.

"You warming up a bit now?"

"Yes—I can't remember when I was ever so cold," she answered. "Soon as my clothes are ready to put on, I'll see if I can find something for us to eat."

"Won't have time for that," Tom said. "I'll boil up some coffee. It'll have to do for a while. By then your clothes ought to be dry and we can move on." He turned his eyes to the east. "Going

126

to be daylight pretty soon and we best be on our way by then."

"The sun will feel so good," Lucilla said. "I'll never complain about it being hot again!"

Bending down, she picked up several branches and added them to the diminishing fire. Medley had crossed again to where the horses were standing. Unbuckling one of the saddlebags, he obtained the tin in which to make coffee along with the lone cup and, from the flour sack, the jar of already ground coffee beans. Setting them near the fire, he unhooked his canteen from his saddle and assessed its contents. It was almost empty. Lucilla's proved in like condition. Emptying both into the tin, he placed the makeshift pot upon two rocks at the edge of the fire and hung the canteens over a shoulder.

"Have to fetch water," he said, mounting the bay and heading out of the clearing. "I won't be gone long."

It took something less than a half-hour. Utilizing a small backwater off the river, Tom was able to brush aside silt and bits of floating trash and fill both containers, but more important, he had a long look at the Pecos, searching for any signs of Hazelwood and his partner as he sought to learn if they had crossed over during the early hours or, as he'd hoped and expected, were waiting for daylight, when it would be safer to ford the rushing stream.

Apparently they had chosen the latter course.

He could see no sign of anyone on this side of the Pecos, but detected what he believed to be a thin streamer of smoke rising in the predawn murk on the opposite bank of the river near where travelers customarily crossed.

"Pretty certain they're still on the other side," he told Lucilla when he returned to the clearing, and detailed why he had come to such conclusion.

The girl's smile reflected her relief. "Then we can get a start on them. Coffee's ready—and some of my clothing is dry. I've already put them on."

"Fine," Medley said. He still felt damp, but because he had moved about, his clothes were in a fairly satisfactory and comfortable state.

Lucilla had drunk her cup of coffee, and taking up the tin and the cup she had used, Tom poured the remaining contents, still scalding hot, into it; then taking a sip at a time, he got it down. While he was thus occupied, Lucilla gathered up the remainder of her clothing, returned again to the back side of the suspended blanket, and completed dressing.

Within a quarter hour they had packed up and were on their way, bearing due east until, as Tom explained to her, they reached a town or familiar landmark that would tell him where they were and the more or less exact direction in which Abilene lay. East—of that he was aware—but they could be far below or well above the settlement and he was eager to follow as direct a route to it as possible.

The sunrise that morning was another vivid display of red, yellow, orange, and salmon colors, all of which hung for a time beneath drifting puffs of clouds and then disappeared into a fan of pearl at the base of which the sun soon appeared and began to spread its welcome warmth over the land.

Lucilla and Medley rode mostly in silence throughout the morning, each occupied with thought, but around noon, when they reached a small town where a halt was made to replace their water-destroyed supplies, a change took place. It occurred an hour or so later when, throwing caution to the wind, they halted on the shady side of a butte and ate a much-delayed meal. Lucilla, bright and cheerful, had turned to Tom.

"You've never mentioned anything about a wife. . . . Are you married?"

Medley took up the small coffeepot purchased, along with another tin cup, a bottle of disinfectant and a can of ointment for his wounds, at the general store just visited, and refilled the container.

"Nope, just never got around to it, I reckon—"

Lucilla settled back, relieved. "Maybe you've never met the right woman."

"Could be. Always figured marriage was something mighty serious—something that lasts for good—not just some kind of a game. Never have found a woman I'd be willing to stick with that long, seems."

Lucilla smiled. "I look at it the same way—and it was like that with my folks. Only after Pa died, Ma had to marry again. Wasn't anything else she could do."

"Country's plenty hard on a woman alone, all right," Medley agreed, staring into the fire. "My ma was dead at thirty-five."

"That's young even for out here!"

"Guess it is," Medley said, and let the matter drop. "Been watching our back trail. Ain't seen nothing of Sid and that other jasper."

"Could they have gotten off on another trail?" Lucilla wondered, beginning to collect the dishes and pans in preparation to leave.

"Doubt it. If they didn't know we were heading for Abilene, I'd say they might, but the way it figures, they're bound to be back there on the main road somewhere."

"I wish they hadn't seen us cross the river," Lucilla said wistfully. "They'd still be there at the ford waiting for us to show up—and we wouldn't have to worry about them."

Tom rolled himself a cigarette from his new sack of tobacco and sheaf of brown papers. "We've got a good start on them, so there's no need to fret about them now. Like as not we'll beat them to Abilene—maybe by as much as half a day." He hesitated, struck a match to his cigarette, and puffed the thin cylinder into life. "You never said anything about it, but are you married to somebody?"

Lucilla's shoulder stirred beneath the rough shirt she was wearing. "No—for the same reason you gave: I never met the man I wanted. Sid tried to marry me off to Red Mescole, but I wasn't about to go for that. Are we very far from Abilene?"

"Three days, maybe closer to four. Tomorrow we'll be in Texas."

"Texas," the girl echoed absently. "I've never been there, but I've heard what fine country it is."

"Can say this about it," Medley replied, rising and preparing to ride out. "It's big."

15

They pressed on for the remainder of that day, crossing a vast, quiet land of plains, shallow swales, and red-banked arroyos. The sun was out, strong, and though the heat was not punishing, it became somewhat uncomfortable. By midafternoon both Lucilla and Tom had taken off their jackets and several times found it necessary to mop at the sweat on their faces and remove their hats to let the faint breeze riffle their hair.

Medley continually maintained a watch on their back trail for indications of Hazelwood and Payton, who most certainly would have crossed the Pecos by that hour and would be now in pursuit. Failing to locate the girl and him once past the river, they most likely had struck out immediately on the main road, for traveling on it would be much faster than on a side trail. Doubtless, they had hopes of overtaking Lucilla and him before reaching Abilene; however, should they not, the pair knew they would all end up finally in the settlement.

Well after dark, Medley and the girl pulled to a stop on the east side of a bluff and made camp. Lucilla had lapsed again into a silence, one that held throughout the meal and evening until they were in their blankets lying on opposite sides of the fire. Only then did she speak.

"Tom, your place—you haven't said much about it."

"Can't say that it amounts to anything right now," he replied, sitting up and rolling himself a smoke. "Got a few cows and steers. Selling off a couple of dozen this year so's I can get my hands on a little cash money. Aim to make some improvements."

Lucilla was quiet while he reached for a glowing brand at the edge of the fire and held it to the tip of his cigarette.

"The house—what's it like?" she continued when that was done.

"Only a couple of rooms. It's plenty run-down, but it'll do me until I can really get into the cattle business, which'll take a few years, I expect. Kind of putting all my attention on doing that right now."

"I guess your taking time off to run down those horse thieves for your friend makes it bad for you."

He shrugged, blew a small cloud of smoke into the warm, night air. "Man has to stand by his obligations," he said. "Wasn't for Cord, I'd not be around at all."

"You could have turned it all over to the law in that town—whatever it's called—"

"Waggomann."

"There was another one, too, the place where we met."

"Bear Springs. Yeh, reckon I could, but I wouldn't've felt right. Amos asked me to do it."

"And you just dropped everything, and did—"

Tom made no comment. He could not see why Lucilla was so taken by the fact he'd chosen to repay a favor. To his way of thinking it was a normal, natural thing to do, and it would have never entered his mind to shift the chore to some lawman, or anyone else.

"Will you lose out on anything, being gone so long?"

"I'm hoping not. Got a boy who lives not far from my place to look after things for me—even having him drive those steers I aim to sell over to a rancher friend who'll get them to the railhead for me—and that's the important thing that had to be done. May lose a few calves, but there'll be another crop next year."

"Sounds like you really love your life—your ranch," Lucilla said. There was a note of sadness in her tone. "Having something to tie down to—call your own—makes a big difference."

Tom Medley nodded. He could understand how and why she felt as she did. Her mother, widowed while Lucilla was yet a child ... then Lucilla becoming the outside member of another family when her mother remarried and thrust her into an unsettled, precarious way of life ... it was little wonder she longed for a decent, permanent home.

He knew a little about loneliness, too. His mother dead when he was barely into his teens, his father disappearing abruptly, he had been on his own almost from childhood. He knew only too well the feeling of always being the stranger, and it had scarred him just as it had marked Lucilla Kinkaid.

He wished he could help her in some way, and gave brief thought to asking her to marry him—an idea that had occurred with increasing frequency to Medley in the past few days. It was no good. He had nothing to offer that could in any way compare with what her relatives in Fort Worth could provide.

He was pleased that Lucilla would at last have a decent place to live, one where she'd no longer fear for her safety and well-being, could lead a normal life and eventually meet a man who could give her the kind of marriage she was entitled to. Tom stirred uncomfortably at the thought and flipped the now-dead cigarette into the lowering fire. He envied that man, whoever he might be. Lucilla was not only a beautiful woman, but a capable one as well.

He started to speak, to say more to the girl and comfort her as best he could, but when he looked he saw that she was sleeping, her features quiet and gentle in repose. A lock of dark hair had come loose from the folds gathered about her head and lay like a feathery shadow on her cheek.

Tom had a sudden urge to rise, to go to Lucilla, to awaken her and tell her how he felt and ask her to be his wife. But caution and better judgment stayed the impulse. He had been over the idea in his mind several times before, and on each occasion had convinced himself that not only was it impractical but it would be unfair to her.

Lying back, Medley stared up into the star-filled sky—a wide, arching umbrella of black velvet shot with sparkling diamonds. Off in the distance several coyotes were burdening the stillness with their discordant complaints, and in the dry brush nearby a small animal of some sort was rustling about in the dry leaves. One of the horses shifted and stamped wearily, and then the next thing Tom became aware of was that it was first light, time to rise and make ready to hit the trail.

They made good time that day as the horses had no difficulty in maintaining a good pace across the mostly flat plains country. At Lucilla's insistence they halted long enough in a small town for her to visit the general store and purchase a new roll of bandage which she immediately used on his wounds. They were all but healed, Medley protested, but the woman would listen to none of that: and when they rode on, both his head and arm injuries were not only properly doctored, but wore clean bandages as well.

Camp that night was on the outskirts of another settlement, and since there had been no indication of Hazelwood and Payton anywhere near their trail, and since there seemed little point now in trying to overtake Rufe Donner and Ike Trigg and the copper-dun stud they had stolen, Tom treated Lucilla and himself to a good supper in the town's one restaurant.

They covered ground equally well the following day, making camp at sunset on the banks of a creek that afforded them a supply of fresh if somewhat evil-smelling water. By that time Tom Medley had his bearings and knew exactly where they were; they had come in far above where he had planned, and so that succeeding morning, with the sky banked with threatening clouds, he veered to a southeasterly course, using the creek itself as a guide.

"In Texas now," he remarked to Lucilla near the end of the day. "See any difference?"

She laughed, a bright, lighthearted sound that brought a grin to his now-bearded face.

"Not one whit—"

"You'd never make a Texan believe that," he said, discarding the bandage about his head since it was no longer necessary. The one on his arm he'd leave undisturbed, since it was not visible. "Ain't nothing nowhere good as old Steve Austin's home ground to hear them tell it.

Camp that night was pleasant, and with sunrise they again mounted and continued on, following the creek for half the day and then again changing course, this time heading due east until they came to a river.

"Folks call it the Colorado," Medley explained. "We'll stay with it for a piece, then cut over toward a town called River Fork. After that we'll come to Colorado City. Was a Texas Ranger headquarters a few years ago, besides being a real wild place. When we—"

"Is there a U.S. marshal there?"

Tom studied the girl for a few moments. She was looking straight ahead as if not wanting to meet his eyes or undergo any questioning.

"Doubt it. Pretty sure there's not one this side of Abilene," he replied, wondering why she wanted to see a federal lawman when any town marshal or sheriff could take care of Hazelwood and Payne.

"I see. How far is Abilene from here?"

"Not much more'n a day's steady ride. Probably take us a bit longer, figuring the shape our horses are in."

Horses . . . That brought to Tom's mind Amos Cord's copper-dun stud—the reason for him being there on the Texas plains in the first place. He still believed he'd find Donner and Trigg in Abilene with the prize horse, hoped he would not learn that the two men, failing to sell the stud as planned, had moved on.

Should the latter prove to be the case, he had no choice but to continue the chase, but if they were yet in the settlement, it would mean the end to the long pursuit and the start of his return home.

It meant something else, too, he realized soberly. Lucilla and he would part, he to go his way while she went on to Fort Worth, where she'd make a new home with relatives. Medley swore softly. It was a depressing thought.

16

Abilene. Nothing appeared to have changed since he was there last. It had been a somewhat new settlement then, thrown together by cattlemen—who needed a shipping point on the railroad for their beef—in a cluster of ironwood, mesquite, oak, and chinaberry trees growing in a hollow among the grassy hills.

The black lava-rock country to the south was just as he recalled; the red soil, the like colored bluffs, the short hills with their rambling patches of prickly-pear cactus, also were familiar. Nor was there a noticeable difference in the settlement itself—the same two-story hotel, the line of low, flat, and slanted-roof buildings that lined the street; the Yellow Rose Saloon, now with three or four competitors; Kelly's Livery Stable, Barnett's General Store, the cattle pens and loading chutes.

"Where's the marshal's office?" Lucilla asked as

they pulled to a stop at the hitch rack fronting the hotel.

Tom had all but forgotten the woman's desire to see a lawman, his mind so firmly set on finding Donner and Ike Trigg and reclaiming the copper-dun stud.

"Right over there—on the other side of the bank," he replied, pointing down the fairly busy street. "You want me to go with you?"

Lucilla dismounted, wrapped the buckskin's reins around the crossbar of the rack. "No, you go ahead with what you have to do—I won't be gone long. Where can we meet?"

Medley, on the ground also and securing the bay beside the buckskin mare, gave that thought. "Stay at the marshal's office. I'll come by there."

Lucilla nodded and turned away. She took only a few steps and halted. Her eyes were filled with concern.

"Tom—be careful," she cautioned.

He grinned. "Same goes for you. We don't know where Hazelwood and his friend are. Could be right here in town." Medley paused, frowned. "Maybe I best go along with you."

"I'll be all right," Lucilla said. "They wouldn't try anything here—not in front of all these people on the street."

Tom glanced about. There were perhaps a dozen persons abroad, about half of whom were women; and the lawman's office was only a short distance away.

"Suit yourself," he said with an offhand gesture. "But stay inside like I said until I come for you. Savvy?"

"I savvy," Lucilla responded with a smile, and moved on.

Medley remained where he was on the strip of board sidewalk in front of the hotel waiting for Lucilla to turn into the marshal's office. When that was done, he came about, mounted the steps to the landing, crossed, and entered the hostelry.

Striding past the deserted lobby with its big leather chairs and shining brass cuspidors, its thick-legged library table upon which were scattered magazines and newspapers, Tom drew up before the desk. An elderly clerk seated on a stool was leafing through a mail-order-company catalog. He looked up when Medley rapped on the counter, and then got lazily to his feet.

"You wanting something?"

"Looking for two men," Tom stated. "One's named Rufe Donner. Other one'll be Ike Trigg. They staying here?"

The clerk leaned back against the wall behind him and pushed his steel-rimmed glasses up onto his forehead. "Who wants to know?"

"I do," Medley snapped impatiently, and reaching out, picked up the hotel's room register.

"Here—you can't do that!" the clerk shouted, lunging forward and making a grab for the book.

Tom stepped away, escaping the man's outstretched arm. "If you'd answered my question instead of flapping your smart lip, I wouldn't have to do this."

Turning slightly to allow the light coming in from the street to fall upon the smudged page, Medley ran a finger down the list of those registering within the last day or two. Immediately he found the names of the two horse thieves. They had signed in three days earlier.

Laying the book on the counter, Tom put his attention again on the clerk, who had backed away and, features sullen, was once more leaning against the wall.

"Pair I'm looking for are here, all right. Room Ten, the book says. They in there now?"

"You're so goddamn high and mighty, maybe you best go see for yourself," the clerk replied angrily.

Medley shrugged, glanced about for a hallway, and locating it headed down its narrow length. Room 10 was the last on the right-hand side, and halting before it, he drew his gun and knocked. There was no answer. Grasping the white china knob, he turned it and pushed gently. The door gave. Hesitating for only a moment, Tom threw the panel wide and stepped quickly into the room.

Trigg and Donner weren't there. Clothing lay about on the two chairs, an empty whiskey bottle stood on the dresser, and the unkempt condition of the bed indicated the horse thieves had been there as recently as that previous night. It was a big relief to know they were still in Abilene.

Doubling back to the lobby, Medley threw a glance at the clerk, who met the look with a sly, smug smile and turned away. There was little use in wasting more time seeking information from him, Tom concluded; the thing to do was have a look in the next most logical place; the town's largest saloon, the Yellow Rose.

Medley returned to the street and, stepping down into the loose dust, struck a direct course for the saloon some distance down the way and on the opposite side. When he drew abreast the marshal's office, the screen door flung open and Lucilla came running to meet him.

"Everything's all taken care of," she exclaimed. "The sheriff—there's a sheriff here, not a town marshal—has already gone over to the railroad office to send a telegram!"

Slowing, Medley stared at the woman, puzzled. He had no idea what she was talking about, but it had to do with Sid Hazelwood and John Payton, he assumed, but other than that he was wholly in the dark.

"Ain't for sure what—" he began.

"Did you find out anything about those horse thieves?" she cut in, more interested in his problem than her own. "Are they still in town?"

"Putting up at the hotel," Tom said, "but they're not in their room. Was heading for the Yellow Rose. Figured they'd likely be there."

"I'm glad they're still around," Lucilla said, features mirroring the relief she also felt. "I was afraid my holding you back on the trail would let them get away. Do you know if they've sold the horse yet?"

So intent was Medley on finding the two men that he had not thought of that. If Donner and Trigg were so bold and confident as to register in at the hotel, they no doubt would stable the copper dun in the town's livery stable rather than leave him hidden somewhere.

"Let's take a look," Tom said, jerking a thumb at Kelly's.

Altering course, they walked hurriedly to the broad, low-roofed barn. The wide front door was open, and entering, they paused in the center of the runway. A man came from a side room nearby, a bit of harness upon which he was working in his hand, and halted.

"You looking to rent a rig or something?"

"No, a friend's horse. Big copper-dun stallion. I think you've got him in here."

"Sure have," the hostler replied, and pointed to the rear of the stable. "Got him in the last stall."

Satisfaction again rolled through Medley. Not only were Trigg and Donner still there, but they hadn't sold the stud. With Lucilla at his side he followed the stableman to the opposite end of the runway.

"Right there," the hostler said. "Sure is a beauty!"

The copper dun had apparently received the best of care, for he appeared to be in excellent condition.

"Your friends are keeping him all spruced up. Had me curry and rub him down. Seems some rancher's coming in to look him over. Aims to buy him if he likes his looks."

"He's beautiful," Lucilla murmured.

Even in the half-light entering the stable through its open doors and dust-streaked windows the coat of the stud glowed like polished bronze. He was holding his head high and proud, and his dark eyes were sharp and bright. For the first time Tom Medley fully understood how Amos Cord felt about the animal.

"When's this rancher coming in? You hear my friends say?"

"Looking for him at the end of the week," the hostler replied. "Whoever he is, he'll sure be a dang fool if he don't buy that horse. There ain't never been nothing like him around here—and he's for certain worth the thousand dollars them boys are asking for him."

"Is for sure," Medley agreed. "Was it you that cleaned him up when they first brought him in, or was it somebody else?"

"Was me. I—"

"There any cuts or bruises on him?"

"Nope, not that I seen. Was a mite dirty—mud and such, but nothing else. They must've been real careful bringing him from wherever they was from. Guess they didn't want him skinned up none on account of that hurting the selling price."

146

"Expect you're right," Tom said. "You got any idea where Ike and Rufe are now?"

"Can find them in one of three places," the stableman said. "Here, the hotel sleeping, or at the Yellow Rose playing cards—they're great ones for that. This here time of day that's where they'll be, I'd bet."

"Obliged," Medley said, and wheeling, returned to the street.

With Lucilla at his shoulder he started again for the Yellow Rose. It occurred to him once more that he was still much in the dark as far as the girl, the outlaws Hazelwood and Payton, and now the sheriff of Abilene were concerned; and he'd like to hear Lucilla's explanation, but it would have to wait until later. His business with Donner and Trigg came first.

Reaching the saloon, they stepped up onto the landing. He faced the woman. "Best you wait out here. I'm looking for trouble from this pair."

Lucilla shook her head firmly. "That's the reason I'm going to be with you," she replied, and touched the butt of the pistol thrust under the waistband of her trousers. "You stood by me against Sid and the others, only right I stand by you. Anyway, we've come this far together—be foolish to split up now."

Tom frowned. He was both pleased and irritated by Lucilla's attitude. It made him feel good that she was willing to back his play, but she could get hurt and he didn't want that. Medley started to protest, to order the girl to remain there on the porch of the Yellow Rose, and then hesitating, he shrugged. He had been with her long enough to recognize the straight-line set of her lips and the look of determination he saw in her eyes.

"All right," he said, yielding, "but remember this, stand clear of me if it comes down to shooting."

Moving on to the batwing doors, Tom shouldered their way through them into the noise and mixed odors that filled the room. Not seeing either of the two men among the customers at the bar who turned to look, Medley glanced about. A hard smile pulled at his mouth. Donner and Trigg were there—sitting at a table playing poker just as the hostler at Kelly's had predicted.

17

Reaching down, Tom Medley let the fingers of his right hand wrap loosely about the butt of the forty-five on his hip and lift it slightly to make certain the weapon was free in the holster. Then, moving deliberately and coolly, still ignoring the men at the bar, he headed for the table where Rufe Donner and Ike Trigg were engaged with three other players in a game of cards.

A stride or two away Medley halted. He cast a glance to one side, making certain of Lucilla Kinkaid's location. Obedient, the girl was off to his left and out of the line of fire.

"Rufe!" Medley called sharply, putting his attention back on the men at the table.

The outlaw looked up questioningly. A frown crossed his whiskered features. "Yeh?" he answered.

Donner didn't recognize him, Tom realized, which was to be expected. He had seen the man only two or three times in his life, and now with a couple of weeks' growth of beard on his usually clean-shaven face, it was little wonder he was a stranger to the horse thief.

"Name's Medley," Tom said. "I'm a friend of Amos Cord. Came after you and Trigg—and the horse you stole."

A heavy silence had fallen over the saloon. The patrons at the bar had stepped back to where they had a better view, and over in the opposite corner of the big room where two of the gaudily dressed girls were sitting with several men, the laughing and talking had hushed and the women were getting to their feet and moving hurriedly away.

"I'm taking you and Trigg there and the stud back to Amos. On your feet—and do it slow and easy!"

Donner, a dark, sly man with small light-colored eyes, forced a tight smile. "That horse is mine, mister," he said. "Ain't you or no other jasper going to take—"

In that same instant Donner lunged to his feet. He brought his gun up fast and fired. In a fraction of time later Medley, surprised, got off his shot. Rufe Donner jolted as Tom's bullet drove into him. He staggered, fell back into his chair, a dazed look on his slack features.

Medley, pistol now leveled at Ike Trigg, determined not to be caught napping a second time, kept his attention on the younger man. Donner's bullet, triggered in too much haste, had missed and buried itself in the far wall of the saloon. He'd been lucky, Tom realized. In his anger at Donner for what he'd done to Amos Cord, he'd gotten careless. It wouldn't happen again.

"You're next—if that's what you want," he called softly to Trigg.

Ike's face drained suddenly of color. Raising his hands, he wagged his head.

"Not me! I ain't about to go for no gun. Hell, I didn't want in on this with Rufe in the first place."

"You were just the same. You and Donner jumped Cord, an old man, shot him, beat him, and left him for dead. You then robbed him of what money he had and stole his best horse, figuring to sell it to some rancher here in Abilene."

"Wasn't no idea of mine," Trigg declared. "Was—"

"It's the truth, though."

"Yeh, yeh, but it was Rufe that done all the planning and such. I just throwed in with him on it. Said he'd kill me if I didn't."

A tall, graying man in a dark suit and high-crowned hat detached himself from the group gathered near the end of the bar. Stepping up to Tom, he nodded curtly.

"I'm T. J. Johnson—with the Texas Rangers," he said, and continued on to where Donner lay half on, half off the chair he'd fallen back into.

The lawman made a quick examination of Rufe, drew his lean frame erect, and faced Medley.

"He's dead. Bullet from your gun took him right

in the heart. Now, who are you and where are you from?" he added, circling the table to Ike Trigg.

"Tom Medley from the Mogollon country over New Mexico way."

"Near what town?" Johnson continued, pulling Trigg to his feet and disarming him.

"Waggomann. What I said about these two men is true. You can get in touch with the marshal there. Name's Teasdale, or you can find out from Amos Cord. He's the man they worked for and that owns the copper dun."

"Don't figure it'll be necessary," Johnson said. "This one here shooting off his mouth like he did is all the proof I reckon I need."

Tom made no comment as he reloaded his gun and slid it back into the holster. Tension was draining slowly from him, and the shock of having to kill a man—even one like Rufe Donner—was having its strong dispiriting way with him. He cast a glance at Lucilla Kinkaid waiting quietly nearby. She gave him a reassuring smile. He turned then to the ranger.

"Glad to hear that. I'd like to get the horse—he's down in Kelly's stable—and head back to Waggomann with him and Trigg—"

"You're welcome to the horse," Johnson said, "but there's no call for you to bother with Trigg. We hang horse thieves here in Texas same as you do in New Mexico."

Someone in the saloon laughed, breaking the tight hush. A voice called for a drink all around, and the ranger, producing a pair of chain-connected handcuffs, affixed them to Ike Trigg's wrists and started for the door with him.

"Be mighty obliged if a couple of you gentlemen would tote the dead man over to Carney's," he said over a shoulder. "Tell Abe I'll drop by later and square up the burying fee."

Tom felt Lucilla's hand upon his. He glanced at her. She was smiling but there was still a hint of brightness in her eyes that betrayed the moments of excitement and fear she had experienced.

"I'm glad you're all right," she said quietly. "When he jerked out his gun and fired, I—"

"Just about made my last mistake that time," Tom agreed wryly. "Should've expected it from Rufe, but I was looking for Trigg to start the fireworks—he's supposed to have been the pistoleer. Donner sort of fooled me."

"I'm glad it's all over. Now you can return the horse to your friend and tell him the thieves have been taken care of."

"And you can go on to your people in Fort Worth—"

Lucilla was silent. One of the saloon girls came up, a glass of whiskey in her hand. She offered it to Medley.

"Man there at the bar—name's Evans—wants to buy you a drink."

Medley accepted the shot glass of liquor, followed the girl's pointing finger to a tall, clean-shaven, well-dressed individual in cattleman's clothing who smiled and raised his drink in salute.

"To all dead horse thieves," he called.

"May we never run out of hanging rope," Tom replied, raising his voice to be heard above the hubbub, and then downed the whiskey. Returning the empty glass to the saloon woman, he put his attention back on Lucilla.

"Expect the next thing we'd better do is take our horses over to the livery stable. They need a good graining and some rest. . . . You aiming to make the ride alone to Fort Worth, or are you going to wait and join a party heading that way?"

They had reached the swinging doors and were stepping out onto the landing of the Yellow Rose. Several men and a few women were standing about in the bright sunshine, evidently discussing the shooting in the saloon, for most fell silent and merely watched when Tom and Lucilla appeared.

"I—I won't be going to Fort Worth," the girl said hesitantly.

Medley studied her narrowly. "Sort of had a hunch that'd happen. Why did you tell me you were?"

They were stepping down into the street and turning to make their way to the buckskin mare and the bay at the rack fronting the hotel.

Lucilla's shoulders stirred. "It's a long story," she said. "We can go into it now, or maybe, after we've taken the horses to the stable, we can go to the hotel, where we can talk without a lot of people around."

Tom Medley, his features stiff, considered the girl more closely. She had lied to him, used him—and although he'd suspected as much earlier, now, knowing it was true not only angered but cut him deeply.

"We'll take care of the horses first," he said gruffly, and reached for the bay's reins.

18

Under the curious gaze of the people scattered along the street Medley and the girl mounted their horses and, wordless, rode to the livery stable. Turning into the runway, they pulled to a halt as the same hostler—Kelly, Tom assumed—came forward to meet them.

"Howdy, folks," he greeted.

Tom merely nodded as he swung down from the bay. Lucilla, also dismounting, smiled faintly.

Kelly, sensing the air of tension between them, reached for the reins of the bay and the buckskin mare. "How long'll you be leaving these horses?"

"Not sure about the lady," Medley replied, "but I'll be riding out in the morning. Want that copper-dun stud ready to go with me."

The hostler frowned. "Well, now, I don't know about that. That horse belongs to them other two fellows—the ones that brought him in. Unless they—"

"Both horse thieves," Tom cut in. "One's dead and the other one's in jail, waiting for a hanging. If you've got any doubts about it, go see that Texas Ranger, Johnson, or the sheriff."

The hostler shrugged. "Sheriff ain't in town. Come got his horse so's he could ride out to the Cameron place after Carl—he's the telegraph operator. Sheriff's wanting to send out a telegram. Maybe it's about them two you're talking about?"

"Not likely," Medley said, and let the matter end.

The stableman, still somewhat confused, turned to Lucilla Kinkaid. "What about you, missy? You be wanting to pull out, come morning, too?"

The girl was silent for several moments and then shook her head. "I'm not sure—I'll have to let you know later."

"Yes'm, whatever you say. I'll just go right ahead and grain and water her just like I aim to do the bay—"

Tom had moved on down the runway for another look at the copper dun. The stud, tall and vibrant-looking in his head-high stance, was more like a bronze statue of a horse than an animal alive.

"I'll be wanting a blanket for the stud," he said as Kelly, leading the bay and buckskin, paused nearby. "One of those strap kind that can be buckled on to stay in place."

"Hell, you won't need no blanket for him, mister," the hostler countered. "Them off-colored chestnuts don't sunburn bad."

"Know that," Medley said irritably. "Get the blanket for him anyway.

He could have explained his idea was to make the copper dun less conspicuous during the long journey back to the Mogollons, but his mood was such that he was short on patience and courtesy.

"Go talk to that ranger if you've got any doubts about me taking the horse," Medley said. "I don't want anything getting in the way of me leaving at first light."

Ignoring whatever reply the stableman made, Tom came about, rejoined Lucilla, and headed back up the runway. They'd go to the hotel, he had decided, and rent a room. Then in private, he'd sit the girl down and find out just what she had been up to and why she had not only used him but also lied to him. It didn't really matter all that much now that it was over and done with, but pride was having its way with Tom Medley and he'd never rest until he knew the truth.

Abruptly he came to a stop. There was no need to go to the hotel, or anywhere else. What was to be said could be said right there in the livery barn. The hostler was well beyond earshot, busy at looking to the needs of the buckskin mare and the bay, and would pay them no attention. Grasping the girl's arm, he turned her about to face him.

"I want to know what's been going on—why you lied to me! And why—"

"Don't go to no bother, cowboy," a voice cut in

from the doorway. "And don't get no ideas about going for your gun."

Tom and Lucilla swung their attention to the stable's entrance. It was Sid Hazelwood. Standing beside him, glancing up and down the street as if making certain there would be no interference, was John Payton.

"Took right smart hustling to catch up with you, sister," Hazelwood drawled, moving deeper into the stable, "but we done it—just like you knew we would."

Payton, now entering the barn, took up a position near Sid and called out to the hostler.

"You—back there in the barn! Get up here—pronto," he yelled, motioning with his pistol.

Kelly complied quickly, coming at a fast walk. Surprise and wonder filled his eyes when he halted. "What the hell—"

"Just stand there and keep your mouth shut," Payton snarled, "unless you want me to blow your damned head off! And you," he added to Medley, again waving the gun in his hand, "pull your iron real slow and throw it over there against the wall."

"Better do it," Hazelwood warned quietly when Tom made no move to disarm himself. "Payton kind of goes a mite looney when he's holding a gun."

Tom drew his forty-five slowly, let it drop to the dirt floor of the stable, and then with the toe of his boot nudged it toward the wall. With the outlaws both leveling their weapons at him, he had no choice but to do as he was told. But, given the slightest chance, he could make a grab for the forty-five, and . . .

"No need to hurt him," Lucilla said. "I didn't tell him anything."

Hazelwood laughed. "I just bet you didn't! Been riding and sleeping with him for a couple of weeks or so, and you didn't tell him nothing about the money! Hell, if you expect me to believe that, then you must figure I believe in Santy Claus!"

"He doesn't know anything," Lucilla repeated stubbornly. "Only who I am and who you are."

"Don't matter nohow," Payton stated. "What we're wanting is what you know."

"John's right," Hazelwood agreed. "Where did you hide the money?"

Understanding was beginning to dawn on Tom Medley. Lucilla had been in on the robbery with her stepbrother and his two partners. They had entrusted her with the stolen cash but she had evidently double-crossed them, and after hiding the money—undoubtedly intending to go back someday when all had quieted down and get it— she had fled. That was when the girl had come to his room that night in Bear Springs and begged to accompany him to Abilene—on her way to Fort Worth, she had said.

It also explained why she had never gotten around to explaining anything to him, even when he had made it a point to question her about what she was running from and why she avoided lawmen.

She had been clever—somehow always managing to dodge giving the answers he had asked for.

"Where you'll never get it," Lucilla replied coolly, folding her arms across her chest.

Tom remembered in that moment the girl was carrying the pistol he had given her earlier. As she was wearing a jacket, it was not visible to the outlaws. Small tags of worry began to pull at Tom. He hoped Lucilla would not try to use it against the two men—she'd not stand a chance; but if he could somehow get the weapon from her . . .

"I ain't swallowing that," Hazelwood said. "You've got it stashed somewhere, and you and your cowboy friend there are aiming to go back for it. Well, guess again—if me and Payton can't get it, you sure'n hell ain't going to either!"

"I told you Tom doesn't know anything. I never let him in on it because I didn't want him to get hurt."

"Him getting hurt!" Payton shouted. "Tell that to Red, laying out there, buzzard meat. Was this here Tom of yours that put old Red under."

"And him doing that sure don't stack up for true to you saying he ain't in on it with you," Hazelwood said.

"He's not," Lucilla repeated, "and anyway, you can forget the money. I've turned it in to the law."

Hazelwood's eyes narrowed. "You bulling me?"

"It's the truth. I waited until I got here and could find a lawman I dared trust. Told him all about the robbery and the killing of that deputy in

Cutterville—and where I'd hid the sack of bank money."

Lucilla turned to Tom. "I didn't tell you about it because you had troubles of your own, and I passed up the lawmen in Bear Springs and those other little towns because I wanted to talk to a U.S. marshal—somebody I could trust. The one in Cutterville was in on the robbery with Sid and Payton and Red Mescole. That made me decide to be real careful who I talked to about it."

"You saying you seen a U.S. marshal here?" Sid demanded, his face coloring with anger.

Lucilla, still calm, her voice even, shook her head. "Was the sheriff—I couldn't find a marshal. But there's a Texas Ranger. The sheriff and him are getting together on it. They're sending a telegram to the U.S. marshal nearest to Cutterville with the information I gave the sheriff. Expect that money'll be back in the bank by morning."

Everything was becoming clear in Tom Medley's mind now. He'd jumped to the wrong conclusions earlier where Lucilla was concerned. He'd thought she was planning to keep the stolen money for herself and had used him to bring it about—but that wasn't it at all. She had simply sought his protection until they came to a town where she could talk to a lawman she believed was honest.

"Maybe you believe all that, but I sure'n hell don't," Payton said, nodding at Hazelwood. "I say we take her back to Cutterville starting right now and make her dig up that sack of money."

"Be a waste of time," the woman said. "It won't be there."

"Maybe—but we'll just go see anyway," Payton said, stepping forward and seizing Lucilla by the arm. "Let's me and you go get your horse."

At that moment Lucilla, brushing up close to Tom, pulled back her jacket. The handle of the pistol she was carrying under her waistband was exposed.

Medley reacted instantly. His hand shot out as the girl lurched against John Payton. Tom's fingers wrapped about the butt of the weapon as Payton, off balance, staggered to one side. Without pivoting, Medley triggered the heavy forty-five. The outlaw, little more than an arm's length away, took the bullet in his chest.

As the impact of the slug slammed Payton against the end of a nearby stall, Tom spun to face Sid Hazelwood. The outlaw had turned, was racing for the doorway. Jaw set, Medley brought up his weapon, leveled the barrel on the man's back, and hesitated. In the next instant Sid Hazelwood had turned into the street and was lost to view.

19

Medley, taut as piano strings, reloaded his gun and walked slowly to the broad opening of the stable. He didn't think the outlaw would press the shoot-out any further, but he had to be sure. Reaching the doorway, Tom threw his glance into the direction Hazelwood had turned. There was no sign of him. Apparently Sid had ducked into the passageway between the stable and its neighbor to the south.

Holstering his weapon, Tom became aware of men running toward him from along the street—among them the ranger.

"What the hell now?" Johnson demanded testily, halting in front of Medley. "You gone and killed another man?"

"In here, T. J.," Kelly called from the stable's runway, and as the lawman entered, the hostler pointed at the body of John Payton. "Was this here dead one's fault. He started it."

Johnson swore, glanced at Lucilla, and nodded slightly in apology. "Getting to be too many killings around here," he commented sourly, and then turned to the stableman. "All right, Ben, tell me what happened."

"Well, the dead man there and his partner had their guns out a-pointing at the big man—"

"Partner?" the lawman interrupted. "There was another one?"

"Sure was," Kelly said. "Took off like a scared rabbit when the shooting started. He get away?" the stableman added, looking at Medley.

"Ducked out of sight," Tom said. "Expect he's already on his way to somewhere."

"Could get up a posse," Kelly suggested hopefully.

"Forget it for now," Johnson said. "Get on with what you were telling me."

"Sure, T.J. Like I said they was a-pointing their pistols at the big fellow. It was all something about a lot of money this here lady had hid somewheres, and they was aiming to take her there so's they could get it. Big fellow somehow got his hands on a gun—I'm danged if I know how—and shot that one there dead. Other'n run like I said. Fellow could have shot him, too, but I reckon he didn't want to put no bullet in his back."

"I see," the ranger said. "Now about this one that got away. Can get up a posse, but I need a reason to bring him in."

"He was in on a bank robbery," Lucilla began, and broke off as Medley shook his head slightly.

There was no reason for her to admit any involvment in the Cutterville holdup. She had been an unwilling partner and had proven so by hiding the money stolen where the outlaws could not get it, and then reported its location to the law so that it could be recovered.

Tom knew enough about the law to realize that if the girl did admit her part in it, even though she was innocent of the crime and would doubtless be cleared of any guilt, such could take days, perhaps weeks, during which she'd probably be confined to a jail cell while the slowly turning wheels of justice cleared her name. And it could yet happen; Medley wasn't sure of where Lucilla stood with the sheriff, of how much she had told him and what his attitude would be.

"I gave all the information I had to the sheriff," Lucilla said, as if in answer to Medley's thoughts. "He was going to send a telegram to a lawman close to the town where it happened, explain it all to him."

Johnson rubbed at his jaw. "I reckon that takes care of things here. Anything you can tell me about the man who run away? You know his name?"

"Sid Hazelwood," the girl replied. "Man there on the floor is John Payton. There was a third man in on the robbery named Red Mescole."

"What happened to him?"

"Shot dead in a gunfight. There's one thing—

and the sheriff knows about it—they killed a deputy when they robbed that bank."

"That sure is a good reason to get up a posse and go after him," Kelly said, again brightening.

The ranger gave that thought. "Yeh, I reckon we could, only that's best left up to the sheriff. I don't want to tromp on his toes."

Tom smiled as he turned to Lucilla. By the time the sheriff, who apparently still hadn't returned to town with the telegraph operator, got the details on Sid Hazelwood, the outlaw would be well on his way back to New Mexico, or perhaps the Indian Territory or a half-dozen other possible directions. About all he'd be able to do then was issue wanted notices for Sid—if he elected to bother with the matter at all. When it was all said and done, the murder of the deputy had taken place in a town over on the New Mexico–Arizona border, and running down the killer was not a concern of the law in Abilene. Eventually, however, some lawman somewhere, someday, would put the cuffs on Hazelwood.

"You fixing to ride out?" Tom heard the ranger ask.

"In the morning," Medley replied. "Got what I came after. No sense hanging around any longer."

"Proud to hear that," Johnson said, an edge to his voice. "We got enough trouble here in Abilene without some outsider shooting up the place."

"Wasn't my choice," Medley said, and taking

167

Lucilla by the arm, started down the street for the hotel.

"I've been wondering about something—you could've shot Sid when he was running for the door," Lucilla said as they walked slowly away from the knot of curious bystanders still collected in front of Kelly's. "Why didn't you?"

"Never was any hand to shoot a man in the back," Tom replied indifferently.

"Even if he was an outlaw—a killer?"

"Still a man just the same—"

"I'm glad you didn't. After all, he was my kin—my stepbrother—the best of the lot. We had fun when we were little kids, and many times he made his brothers leave me alone. It was only after we grew up that Sid got the way he is. Do you think he'll give us—me any more trouble?"

"Hard to say. Sure wasn't showing much brotherly love toward you back there in that stable. . . . What're you aiming to do now?"

Lucilla stared off over the grassy hills beyond the town. Back of the Yellow Rose a dog was barking frantically, and a man and a woman in a red-wheeled buggy was just turning into the end of the street pointing apparently for the general store.

"I was hoping you'd let me ride back with you to New Mexico. There's nothing here for me in Abilene—or anywhere else far as that goes."

Medley's voice was low, reserved. "Guess you're welcome to come along."

She turned her full attention to him. In the bright sunlight her tanned features were strong, and the blue of her eyes was several shades lighter than he recalled.

"It's not right for me to just plain come out and say this, Tom, but can't we get married? I love you—and I'm sure you've come to care for me despite the things that've happened. We could make a good life together on your ranch, and—"

Medley was shaking his head slowly even before the girl could finish. "Nothing I'd like better, but truth is I've got nothing to offer you—not even a decent place to live. Times, too, when I don't even have money to put grub on the table. Maybe, in a few years, if my luck's good—"

"Being hard-up wouldn't make any difference," Lucilla said earnestly. "I'm used to it and I'd be happy to share it with you—"

"No." Tom Medley's tone was flat, final. "I saw my ma die at thirty-five—worn out, worked to death. Not about to let any woman I love in for a life like that."

Lucilla lapsed into silence. They had reached the hotel, had halted at its corner. Then, facing him, she asked, "You ever stop to think that your ma didn't mind the hard times—that she loved your pa so much it didn't make any difference to her?"

Medley's wide shoulders moved slightly. "No. Could be what you're saying's true, but it don't change anything far as I'm concerned. I'll never put the woman who'll become my wife through what she had to put up with. . . . Expect it'll be a good idea for you to get yourself a room here and rest up. I'd like to leave by daylight in the morning."

Lucilla assented woodenly and started up the steps to the hotel's landing. "Where'll you be?"

"First off, I've got to lay in some trail grub and see about a sack of grain for the horses. Can look for me to come by about dark for you. Can go and eat supper at that restaurant down the street—if you'd like."

"I'll be ready," Lucilla said dispiritedly. "Will you be staying here in the hotel tonight, too?"

Tom considered the meaning that lay beneath the question. The girl evidently had some fear that Sid Hazelwood might return and search her out. Tom had his doubts that such would happen, but he didn't want her to worry.

"Figured to—and I'll have the clerk give me the room next to yours just in case you should need something. . . . Been intending to mention this—is it going to be all right with that sheriff for you to leave town in the morning?"

"I asked him that and he said to go ahead, that he had all the information he needed. And since I went to the law on my own and told the whole story—and wasn't really in on the robbery—I wasn't guilty of anything."

"Good—just didn't want any posse dogging us," Medley said with a smile, and moved on.

20

Rested, refreshed, supplies replenished, Medley and Lucilla Kinkaid were up early, had breakfast at the Abilene Home Restaurant, and were on their way back to New Mexico not long after sunrise—the copper-dun stud wearing a new black-and-tan blanket and carrying some of the load.

Tom had succeeded in purchasing an amount of oats for the horses, remembering only too well how poor grazing was in certain areas; and too, he wanted the stud to look as good as possible when they reached Amos Cord's place in the Mogollons. He'd had the feed-store merchant put the fifty pounds of grain in two sacks, which he then fastened together at the necks and hung them across the withers of the stud like a pair of saddlebags.

The horse didn't like the idea much at first, and did his utmost to rid himself of the unaccustomed burden, which Medley had made secure by tying it to the surcingle; but by midday he had accepted the load, light in weight but no doubt strange and annoying to him, as Cord had never broken the animal to anything but a rope halter.

Tom and Lucilla had little to say to each other all during that first day of the long return journey, and their first camp that night was a quiet one, each seemingly wrapped in personal thoughts. However, by the following morning the distance between them had dissipated and they once again were at ease with each other.

"Maybe I can get a job in Waggomann," Lucilla said as they pushed steadily on. "I could be a waitress or work in a dressmaker's shop."

"Sure wish I had the cash—I could set you up in your place," Medley said.

She smiled. "Best you hang on to your cash, get that ranch of yours to going good. Hard as you're working at it, you're entitled to end up big."

Tom thought he detected an undercurrent in her words. "Just wish I felt I could afford a wife," he said. "It would be you for sure, but right now it's not in the cards, and I reckon you know why."

"I know," she murmured, "and while I can't agree, I respect your reasons."

Late that day they encountered a large party of Indians—Comanches, Medley thought. They quickly took cover in the brushy arroyo and waited for the group to pass—no more than a hundred feet or so away. As there were women and children to be seen, along with a number of dogs,

Medley guessed it was a village on the move to a better area.

He was relieved they had seen the Comanches in ample time to hide; had the braves caught sight of the copper dun, they would have demanded the big horse from him—and against such a large number of warriors there'd be nothing to do but surrender the stud.

They ran into rain several days later, which set up a worry in Tom Medley's mind. The Pecos River could still be flooding, as might also the Rio Grande, but to his relief they found the former had receded and they crossed it at the ford with water barely up to their stirrups.

The Rio Grande was down to near normal also when they reached and crossed it, and then late in the morning of the eleventh day since leaving Abilene, they turned into Waggomann's one street.

"I—I guess this is where we part," Lucilla said, pulling to a halt.

He smiled. "I reckon—but just for a spell. You're still aiming to stay in town, find yourself a job—"

"If I can," she replied, glancing around. "I doubt there's very many places here that have work for a woman, except the saloons, and I'd as soon not take a job in one of them."

"No, for sure not," Tom agreed. "You go on over to the hotel, get yourself a room. I'll take the copper-dun stud on to Amos, let him see that everything's all right, then come back. Maybe I

can do a little talking here and there and help you
find something to do."

"That'll be fine," Lucilla said, and turned for
the hotel.

Tom, a heaviness filling him, watched the girl
move off for several moments, and then resumed
the ride up the street. He'd help her find a decent
job of some kind there in Waggomann—he had
friends enough for that. To think of her leaving
was painful; he couldn't imagine what it would be
like not having her around, he'd gotten so used to
her, and he knew he'd miss hearing her voice, her
laugh, and seeing her lovely face while she watched
him at some chore, or her eyes light up when
something he did pleased her.

Maybe he was a damn fool to take the position
he had; maybe, as she had insisted and endeavored to make him understand, a woman in love
with a man didn't mind the hardships and grief
she faced. But he still couldn't accept it. He couldn't
bear to think of her turning old and broken before her time, worn out, her beauty gone, and—

"Tom!"

Medley came to a stop in the center of the street
as town marshal Bert Teasdale emerged at a run
from his office.

"Glad you're back!" the lawman said, grasping
the bridle of the bay. "And I'm damn glad I seen
you before you got by." He paused, flicked a glance
at the copper dun. "See you got Amos' horse back
for him. Too bad."

"Too bad? What's that mean?"

"Got some sorry news for you, Tom," Teasdale continued. "Amos Cord's dead—cashed in a couple of days after you left."

For a long minute Tom sat in stunned silence. Then, "Sure hate to hear that. He was a fine man—I owed him a lot."

"Seems he felt the same way about you. Fact is, he left everything he had—ranch, horses, and all—to you. I've got a paper here—a will, I reckon you'd call it—putting it all down in black and white. Legal, too. I was there when Doc Masters wrote it out for him—and done the witnessing when he signed it.

Tom Medley was having trouble believing what the lawman had said. Amos Cord dead. Now all his old friend owned, the ranch property, the stock of horses including the copper-dun stud, were all his! Cord's place combined with his own spread would add up to a fine ranch, one that in a couple of years could really amount to something.

"Amos left a note for you, too. Says to pick twenty horses—good strong stock—and drive them over to the army at Fort Bayard—they're waiting for them. Amos says to collect forty dollars a head, and that the commandant there'll likely want another twenty horses in a couple of months. Now, if you—"

Tom Medley was no longer listening. He had turned about, was hurrying toward the hotel where Lucilla Kinkaid was in the act of dismounting. She glanced up in surprise as he, all but dragging the copper-dun stud behind the bay, came to a halt before her.

"That offer of yours still open?" he asked, grinning broadly.

"Offer—what," Lucilla began, and then parted her lips in a smile also. "You mean get married—be your wife?"

"Just what I'm meaning—I'll tell you all about it later. Right now we'll get you settled in the hotel, then find us a preacher, then I'll get hold of some hired hands and start fixing up the house so's it'll be a decent place for us to live in. You can live here in the hotel until it's ready."

Medley's words had all come out in a rush. Pausing, he studied the girl closely. "How's that all sound?"

"Sounds wonderful, that's what," Lucilla said, "but I'd sort of like to make a couple of changes."

Medley pushed his hat to the back of his head and frowned. "Changes?"

"Yes, let's find that preacher right now. And to hell with me staying here in the hotel—I'll move out there to your place with you right now."

"Told you before it's not much of a house—"

"We'll make do," Lucilla said lightly. "Anyway, I think a woman ought to be on hand when her home's being fixed up."